DWINDLING

Selected Works by David R. Slavitt

The Outer Mongolian (1973)

Vital Signs: New and Selected Poems (1975)

Dozens (1981)

Alice at 80 (1984)

The Hussar (1987)

Salazar Blinks (1988)

Lives of the Saints (1990)

Short Stories Are Not Real Life (1991)

Turkish Delights (1993)

Crossroads (1994)

The Metamorphoses of Ovid (1994)

PS3569.L3 (1998)

*Get Thee to a Nunnery:
Two Shakespearean Divertimentos* (1999)

The Book of the Twelve Prophets (2000)

The Book of Lamentations: a Meditation and Translation (2001)

Aspects of the Novel: A Novel (2003)

Re Verse: Essays on Poets and Poetry (2005)

Change of Address: Poems, New and Selected (2006)

The Seven Deadly Sins and Other Poems (2009)

The Crooning Wind: Three Greenlandic Poets (2012)

Civil Wars: Poems (2013)

The Jungle Poems of Leconte de Lisle (2014)

Walloomsac: A Week on the River (2014)

The Octaves: Poems (2017)

DWINDLING

a novel by

DAVID R. SLAVITT

newamericanpress

Milwaukee, Wis.

newamericanpress

www.NewAmericanPress.com

© 2020 by David R. Slavitt

Printed in the United States of America

ISBN 9781941561218

Book design by David Bowen

For ordering information, please contact:
Ingram Book Group
One Ingram Blvd.
La Vergne, TN 37086
(800) 937-8000
orders@ingrambook.com

For Janet

TABLE OF CONTENTS

ONE

Novels are in prose. And novelists are pros, at least in the sense that they get paid for their work—or hope to. Poets, for the most part, are amateurs, which is to say that they do what they do for the love of it. If they get paid at all, the amounts are trifling. Insulting, even. They make a living either by teaching or, in the case of Rimbaud, selling guns to various tribes in Africa—he found this to be more interesting than poetry, which he abandoned.

At least in Africa, he could see the lions, the snakes, and the poisonous insects, and none of them smiled at him, the way critics and men of letters did back in Paris. (They bit nevertheless.)

Even so, let us imagine Rimbaud, haggard and hollow-eyed, slogging along by the banks of the dark, gray-green, greasy Limpopo, his guides in front of him and his bearers behind him, and he comes upon… St. Beuve? The Goncourt brothers? (It would have to be both the brothers. Apparently they never spent more than a day apart from each other in their entire lives.) They jump out from behind a tussock to confront him. Does he offer them an aperitif? Or take one of the rifles from stock and blow them away, regretting only that he cannot take their heads back to Kinshasa to have them mounted.

(Is a tussock different from a tuffet? Which is larger?)

On these African ventures, Rimbaud walked. Haggard was mounted as often as possible, which is why he was called Rider Haggard.

Back when he had been living with Verlaine, Rimbaud had also been mounted, but that's another story.

One of the advantages of pointlessness is that it is impossible to wander from a non-existent point or venture off to someplace beside it. This may make a messy kind of book, but it is more true to life, which is also messy and doesn't have a point either. We deceive ourselves if we try to discern a direction in our chaotic experience, as if there were some sort of narrative—with a meaning. Only in hindsight and by distortion can we persuade ourselves that we intended any of the things that happened to us. Some trivial events might have been planned and fulfilled, but even those turn out to be in some measure accidental. The produce section had no parsnips, so I bought garlic instead to put into the mashed potatoes. As far as the larger, more crucial moments, we were often astonished by how things turned out.

Could that little blonde girl in the school orchestra have dreamt of playing the bassoon? Did her parents imagine themselves sitting by the fireside, sipping after-dinner cordials, and listening to her practice solo runs and trills on that dark, reedy instrument (presumably in another room)?

"How did I wind up here?" is a question many of us are sometimes forced (taunted) to ask, and if we are honest in our answers we have to admit that we have no idea. How it happened and what it meant are mysteries because they are grandiose illusions.

Most misleadingly, there can be possibilities of reasons that we think can explain things. The school orchestra's bassoonist graduated last year and there was an empty chair in the woodwinds section. There were many youngsters who hoped to play violins or even, if it came to that, violas, so there was stiff competition for those positions. The music instructor and conductor of the ensemble (less bad than you might have expected) actually needed a bassoonist. He announced this to everyone but only our little girl accepted the bargain, avoiding the stress of having to compete with her classmates but condemning herself to those sounds that a baritone duck might make. How many times will they play "Peter and the Wolf," where the bassoon has a substantial part as the grandfather?

See? The mystery is solved. But is it? How did it happen? This shy young woman's parents thought she might come out of herself a little if she were to engage in some group activity, a sports team or even the school orchestra. And the teacher could just as easily have suggested the tuba—and might have done if he hadn't needed a bassoonist more. (Brasses are largely interchangeable.) Or the family could have bought a house just a few blocks away which would have put them in another school zone with no orchestra but an active theater group. Which among these was the principal cause? We shrug and decide not to decide, which is to say we invoke Fate.

Does Fate intercede in such insignificant developments? That is an absurd question but its absurdity does not affect its legitimacy, does it? Or, for that matter, our answers.

Now where are we? It is probably better to have a spot in which to exist, although one might make the case that existence itself is vulgar. Banal. Plato's idea of a chair has the dignity of never having been fully realized. Aristotle, on the other hand, takes chairs as he finds them, dozens and hundreds of chairs, and generalizes to a concept of chair-ness. But with every flaw or imperfection in every specimen? Thank you, but no. Materiality is inevitably a comedown. Being is a compromise and all compromises are unsatisfactory. The ultimate chair escapes the designer's ambitions and the lomwright's best efforts to float above them in its ideality in an unsullied although probably chilly heaven of abstractions.

"Won't you sit down, Mrs. Gundelfinger?" It's an Actor's Studio exercise, I think. Say that in twenty different ways, conveying a different emotion each time: menacing, subservient, arrogant, bored, relieved, and so on. My point is that you do not have to specify the chair behind her. You suppose there must be one, but its style and condition are of no interest to you. It approaches ideality by its absence; its existence is notional and implied. Do you see? Are you perhaps even beginning to be annoyed? "Won't you sit down, Mrs. Gundelfinger?" this time in a conciliatory, almost sorrowful tone.

We try again, then. Something specific. The last straw on the camel's back that the drowning man clings to. He should instead have clung to the camel, which apparently was able to swim. It could happen. This might have been a lucky camel, or, for all I know, all camels can swim but it is a talent they rarely get to exhibit.

A place, then, which is to say a context. What happens is difficult to understand unless we know where and when the event, as we say, took place. It takes a place for something to take place. Sounds like gibberish but there is a meaning to it, albeit shadowy. (Still, if there are to be shadows, there must be light and objects casting them, even though we may not know what they are.)

How about the Rua dos Douradores? In Lisbon. Douradores are gilders, which is about right, inasmuch as novelists take ordinary things and gild them to make them more attractive and more interesting, even if their nature is changed in the process. Or betrayed. (For fancy editions, the edges of the books' pages may also be gilded.)

The trouble with novelists is that they think too much. Or they think about the wrong things. I have never been able to persuade myself that Billy Budd called out, "God bless Captain Vere!" Gilded horseshit—even though there probably weren't any horses aboard HMS *Bellipotent*. I admit, I had to look that up. And I found out that the ship from which Budd had been impressed was *The Rights of Man*. I'd forgotten that, too. Or rejected it. Melville's brain was up to more mischief than we might have liked.

It is not at all surprising that most of the readers of Herman's books (Hermaneutics?) are undergraduates. Grownups have acquired a distrust of claims of meaning. We surely dislike being beaten on the head and shoulders with the heavy machinery of Significance. A more likely name for the American vessel would have been *Phyllis G*, or some such thing. Whatever the name was of the owner's wife or daughter.

Now, where were we? That was the subject, actually. Where? A place. And I had proposed a street in Lisbon. I have only been in Lisbon once, for a few days as a tourist. That was years ago, and I don't remember much about the place. Hilly, I think. And the streets were clean and the flowers on the traffic islands were well tended. Those are the benefits of dictatorships. I think my visit was after Salazar's death, but habits have a way of hanging on, even good ones. I remember the carved stone knots around some of the windows in what I think was Manueline architecture. Also there were a lot of wooden chickens on people's lawns. But those details are all I can recover from the fog of time. Oh, and a nightclub where there was a gypsy singing Fado. But that's it.

(Wooden chickens? Sim, Senhor! The Galo de Barcelos. You can look it up.)

In other words, Lisbon is a perfect setting for whatever this is. A mostly fictional place that is on actual maps. Like those Italian cities in which Shakespeare set some of his comedies: a notional Verona, a perfunctory Padua, a virtual Venice.

But why that particular street? Because that was where Bernardo Soares lived and worked, that assistant bookkeeper whom we are supposed to think wrote *The Book of Disquiet*, in the same way that we are supposed to think that Ganeesha wrote the *Mahabara-ta*, or at least transcribed it from the god's dictation. I remember it was Ganeesha, the elephant god, because at some point his pen breaks and he pulls out one of his tusks and with it keeps on writing. Sr. Soares I remember because he was so memorably unmemorable—a trick he had spent years perfecting.

The traditional historical novel goes the opposite way. There's a complication which only gets worse, a desperate situation that cannot be resolved, and then, at the last minute and in the last chapter, voilà, in comes the prominent person—Queen Elizabeth, or Napoleon, or I don't know... Trotsky, maybe.

But there the novelist is clinging to the coattails of his character's fame for credibility. It is much more interesting to keep to perfectly ordinary people and let them work out their problems, or fail to, as happens in the real world with Zeno, or Leopold Bloom, or Willy Loman, about whom Arthur Miller declaims in a ringing, self-pitying passive, "Attention must be paid!"

This violation of decorum—and grammar—would never arise in Soares's mind. He'd rather that no attention be paid. Attention is often unwanted, frequently embarrassing, and in any event intrusive. If non-existence is the desideratum, then the next best thing is an almost unnoticed existence, membership in a crowd in which one can conceal himself. (Where's Waldo?)

Let us suppose that you have in some closet a good-sized cardboard box in which you have stored a pile of photographs. They aren't of sufficient interest or value to keep them accessible. On the other hand, they have not descended into (or achieved) the worthlessness that would allow you to trash them. There is, in the carton, a wide group picture of your ninth-grade class. You didn't "graduate" from the ninth grade, but you did progress to senior high school. Some administrator decided that the occasion should be marked, and the photograph must have been part of that ceremony.

Can you find yourself? Are you partially obscured by the boy in front of you who has turned his head? (Good.) But among the others, whom do you recognize? How many can you remember? Your presence in the photograph must be as meaningless to them as their faces are to you. One or two of them you think you knew, but can you recall their names? Their ghostly presences have an aesthetic and even moral attraction. They do not insist upon themselves. Their modest indeterminacy is closer to the truth of life than what most fiction offers us.

The generalization is plausible. The difficulty arises when we try to apply it individually. We suppose ourselves to be the protagonists in our lives. (Are our successes or failures important enough to bear such scrutiny?) Some of us even imagine suitable background music for whatever we are doing. More probably, we are bit players, even extras. Or one of those opera supers who put on costumes and get made up just to be part of an onstage crowd, but we do not have a word to say or a note to sing. All we have to do is come in from there, move there, go there, and then exit. We don't even have to wait around for the curtain calls but can get back into our own clothes, leave the opera house, and take the bus home.

The soprano's passion, the death of the tenor, and the triumph of the wicked baritone may attract the attention of the audiences (and the critics, too) but honestly what has any of that to do with us? We are far better off in the bus in our inconsequential obscurity. We are at least likely to be less miserable than the featured singers are. In their roles and their lives. ("Less miserable" would be a good title for something.)

Think of *Moby-Dick*. (The title is hyphenated, although the whale is not. Well, many people know that, but which of them has any idea what that could mean. The book title would normally be in italics and the whale in Roman type, but Melville must have known that, and therefore he must have meant something else. Or was it just a typo as in *Typee*?) Ishmael, Ahab, and Queequeg are the main characters, but it's Starbuck who survives and, after the voyage, resolves never to go to sea again. Instead, we can think of him opening a successful chain of coffee houses. (Nonsense? But nonsense can be soothing. It can even sometimes be true.)

The ambition Soares has of not having any ambition is only apparently paradoxical. Actually, many people learn to live this way. Just be yourself. Spies of course, and impostors, who make every effort not to be noticed, wrestle with this problem. Not that you or I will be joining some secret service in the immediate future, but there are ways in which we find ourselves recruited. In unpleasant or merely unfamiliar circumstances, one of the ways of retreating is consciously to act the part of yourself. Your life is no longer merely your quotidian existence but rather a performance of what you take to be your rôle. You feel more comfortable as a pretender, less involved and less responsible. Whatever happens was in the script you were handed when you arrived at the theater. Costume and makeup are quite convincing, and you have the accent right, so it is not a difficult part to play. But you do have to appear to be involved, to be listening when the other characters speak, to react with the expected expressions and replies. You get the hang of it, easily enough. And you are just as happy that it isn't a major part. For many of the scenes, you don't even appear on stage.

Your name is not listed in the program. That, too, is pleasing. If they had insisted, you would have provided the management with a stage name. If the mere omission of a name is a zero, the appearance of a pseudonym must be reckoned as a negative quantity. Dark matter, maybe, of which there is supposed to be a great deal in the universe.

Rua dos Douradores is a two-way street. We could make something of that but it would be too easy and, therefore, unworthy of you or me. Cobblestones? Why not, but we must understand that it isn't a deliberate gesture toward quaintness but simply evidence of municipal neglect. No trucks full of asphalt have ever come here to cover the stones with black, tarry stuff that smells bad. (The odor persists for weeks.) At intervals, there are concrete planters with seasonal flowers in them, a leftover nicety from the old days—which historians have named "para-fascist," to try to distinguish the Portuguese from other countries' varieties of nationalist authoritarianism.

The building is five stories high, which means it does not have an elevator. Its exterior is shabby with the stucco missing in places to reveal the brickwork behind it. Bernardo's room is on the top floor, so he gets more than enough exercise on the stairs whenever he goes outside or returns. The room is bare with the walls painted (long ago) in a dull mustard color. Or non-color. It is what bureaucrats often choose for the walls of prisons and high schools. On the contracts, they call it ochre, which sounds better but looks the same.

In most novels, a detailed description like the foregoing (the stucco missing in places!) is a mise en scène, which leads us to expect a scène of one kind or another. We have here not only Chekhov's rifle over the fireplace but the fireplace, too, the room, and even the address. It would be perverse if the curtain were to rise and then nobody made an entrance. Nothing would happen and then the curtain could drop. This is way beyond the Theater of the Absurd. This is the theater of Truth. Most of the time, in real rooms, nothing happens, or surely nothing important enough to record and re-enact. But we can indicate that. Let's put CLOSED FOR RENOVATIONS on the marquee as if that were the title of the production. Or simply FERMÉ. Where the pictures go in the lobby vitrines, we can have random photographs of actors in other plays, as if they had been left from comedies and tragedies that played here years ago.

Anyway, after a reasonable (or, better, unreasonable) waiting time, let's have a cleaning woman come in (left) with a feather duster, make a pass at the bookcase shelves and the writing table, and then exit (again left). With theater tickets at these prices, the audiences deserve to see *something*, don't they? (Well, not really, no. And what does deserving have to do with anything? Do we still believe in the tooth fairy?)

Some of the less sophisticated theatergoers will feel cheated and, even worse, angry because they have been made to look like fools. Shouts, whistles, and catcalls. (Catcalls and whistles are difficult to distinguish). So, you see, something has happened, at least for those of us who can appreciate the wit of nothingness. M. Sartre called it *néant*, which sounds more important, as if there were nuances we don't get from "nothing." But it means the same thing.

Nothing.

Back on the Rua dos Douradores at the building where Bernardo Soares lives, we can see him approaching. Not trudging, exactly, but walking slowly and deliberately. The cobblestones we thought of a while back can be tricky to navigate, especially for the elderly. And Soares is not only elderly but actually "old," which has become a tactless word, except for doctors, who refer routinely to the old and the "old old"—a category we reach when we turn 85. And Soares? As near as I can figure, he must be 137, an unlikely age, but as a fictional character he can survive as long as we want him to. He is older then even than those wrinkled characters in the Caucuses who eat nothing but yoghurt and kale and achieve an astonishing senectitude.

He is coming home from work. He is an assistant bookkeeper in an office just two blocks away. No, I have only a vague idea of what an assistant bookkeeper does, but the title conveys the diffidence Soares prefers. The position must have something to do with ledgers and the entry and manipulation of numbers. This is an anodyne exercise, because if you are doing arithmetic, you are not thinking of anything else. Therapy for the manic and the depressed alike: it cannot cure these disorders (moods? philosophies?), but it can provide remission, suspending for a while all mental activity that is not relevant to the columns of numbers on the paper before you. You can achieve psychic balance as you reconcile the balances in your statement and your checkbook. Come to think of it, the aim of bookkeepers and their assistants is to reach zero, where the assets and the liabilities achieve a delicate equipoise.

Slender and slightly stoop-shouldered, Soares is wearing a black suit—probably the same one he wore back in the thirties when we last saw him. The seat of the pants is now shinier but when he is wearing the jacket, as he is now, we can't see that. His tie is a solid color, purplish in direct sunlight but otherwise black. Is it too fanciful to suggest that he resembles a crane as he negotiates his way over the cobblestones? We can look up at the building and, if we allow him enough time to climb those flights of stairs, we will see a light go on in his window.

Not much in the way of action, is it? But he much prefers it this way. If you do something, you are liable to be found out for having done it. Fingerprints, DNA, and all those fearsome forensics. To avoid notice, then, you should do as little as possible. The lightlier you tread, the sketchier your footprints. Sounds like one of those enigmatic fortunes in the cookies Chinese restaurants give you.

(Okay, but what is your Chinese word on the other side of the slip?)

A bare room, but you could have guessed that. Bed, nightstand, wardrobe, and a writing table next to which is a straight-backed wooden chair. It could be a student's room, except that a student would have put something on the walls, a movie poster maybe, or a print of some painting or other. What they are trying to do is to mark the space as theirs, to claim or sign it. If such an idea were to cross Bernardo's mind, the corners of his thin lips would drop a millimeter or two in an involuntary display of distaste.

On the table are a fountain pen and a notebook of lined, blank paper. Those mark his presence. If the table had a drawer, they would be hidden away, not because anyone visits here but rather because that would be his natural preference.

Every morning he makes his bed, which is another way of removing evidence that someone lives here or at least has slept here.

A small bookcase, of course. And the modest collection of books tells a little about him. (A Portuguese dictionary and a Latin one, as well as a Latin grammar. A few classical poets—Virgil, Ovid, Catullus, and Horace. And several volumes of Portuguese poetry—Cesário Verde, Luís de Camões, Manuel Bandeira—and translations into Portuguese of Tolstoy and Chekhov. But then these are all books any cultivated person would have.)

Were we to open the notebook on the table and peek at a random page, we might be struck by the observation: "I think, therefore I think I am," which is a minimalist assertion (all the more persuasive because it claims less). The handwriting is delicate with small loops in the cursive majuscules, but perfectly legible as we might expect from an assistant bookkeeper.

I think I think. Or I think I think I think. There is an infinite regression as at the barbershop where the mirror before the customer reflects back to the mirror behind him, which of course reflects back ad infinitum. (Odd infitum!) Each head is slightly smaller as one looks ever more deeply into this suggestive declension. The diminution in size could be an indication of the displeasure of each of the figures in what it sees and its desire for further dwindling.

This observation may be momentarily diverting but Soares has not thought it interesting enough to enter in his notebook. But then nothing is, unless it prompts an insight, however trivial. If the mind were sharper, the observations keener, and the soul more responsive, then most of the things one ignores could turn out to be rich with significance. There is, for example, a weed in front of his house, a small plant, five or six inches high, that has struggled to arise from a tiny crack between the wall and the sidewalk. Weeds do that. Do they then deserve criticism for their foolishness in having selected such an improbable spot in which to exist? Or praise for their courage and determination? In millennia, when the jungle has retaken the city, it will be in part thanks to these brave skirmishers who gave their wretched lives so carelessly but who expanded, if only infinitesimally, the width of that barely noticeable fissure.

One cannot talk seriously about the aspirations of a weed, or not an individual weed. But deep in the genetic code, there is an ambition of the whole species to grow and multiply, to turn the street eventually into an Alpine meadow in which this kind of plant has established itself and, in its handsome unanimity, presides. Imagine several acres of buckhorn, for instance. That is the weeds' dream and only aim. The external world doesn't intrude or, insofar as the plant is concerned, even exist. (Does buckhorn grow in Portugal?)

Where would we place such thoughts on the spectrum that runs from idiocy to brilliance?

Do we have to?

Not interesting enough to unscrew the cap of his Pelikan pen, but perhaps sufficiently engaging for him to imagine doing so. Writers write, of course, but they also imagine themselves writing, elegant descriptions of places, faces, and objects. They do not have to bother with the tiresome business of choosing words. They can leap ahead to the effect those words would have, the satisfying vividness it is so difficult to achieve on paper, the elegant simplicity. The admirable paragraphs they thus conjure up are their habit, a voice-over in the bio-pic they fancy themselves to be appearing in. The voice is commenting on the action, perhaps explaining it well enough for the actor/producer/director to understand it. This analysis of what is happening, may not enlighten, but it is flattering and probably soothing. It is a way a person takes notice of his or her existence, which is why there are so many mental poets and novelists.

No editing, no proofreading, no revision, but always perfect, as one never can be at the writing table with its inky actuality.

Smoke rises; fog falls. Sometimes they meet, as if in a rendezvous of complementary hazes. Have I seen this before but not noticed?

Or is it a relatively rare event, like an eclipse, truly a novelty?

It is a question I cannot answer or rather say that I cannot trust whatever answer I propose. Depressed, I blame myself, but in a more cheerful mood I am likely to believe it is a novelty and that it is not my fault for having failed to observe it before. It would be unreasonable to feel guilt about not having noticed that I have not noticed.

(Unreasonable, but not necessarily wrong.)

The more difficult question, which I am not yet able to answer, is whose thought it was about the smoke and the fog. Was this Bernardo Soares speaking or writing in his notebook? Yes, of course, but that's not possible. He is a fiction, as you perhaps divined when I mentioned his age. Yes, but whose fiction is he, Pessoa's or mine? The distinctions get fuzzy, or hazy with the confluescing smoke and fog. Being fictional, he can't die, or if he could and did, then he could be revived, as I have done. Or imagined doing. Like Lazarus he is brought back to life. When he had done this, Jesus called in a loud voice, "Lazarus, come out!" The dead man came out, his hands and feet wrapped with strips of linen, and a cloth around his face. Jesus said to onlookers, "Take off the grave clothes and let him go."

A curious instruction, is it not? Why did they need to be told to let him go? Because as Jesus understood the man was no longer of interest. Not interesting dead or alive, but only during the transformative moment. After that, a mere curiosity, a souvenir, and Jesus didn't want to have the man's life ruined by irrelevant celebrity, as it almost certainly would have been. His sisters, Mary and Martha, were already getting more attention in Bethany than they wanted. So Lazarus became their manager maybe and kept the pestering public at bay.

I doubt that Soares will have that kind of problem. This is a relief, because I don't want him to blame me for what I intended as a kindness. No writer wants to be on bad terms with his characters.

Soares was a stick figure Pessoa dreamed up to hide behind, and if you can hide behind a stick figure you are slender indeed. Almost invisible, which is what Pessoa was aiming for—to be there, but just barely, the unobserved observer, the impersonal personality. In a three-way mirror, you stand there and let the tailor fuss with the shoulders, the length of the sleeves, the positioning of the front buttons, but there you are on that carpeted podium and in multiple. Paradoxically, it is a good place to hide, because you can see many other versions of yourself in the different mirrors (although they will all have the same cuff length).

So, whom do we have here, crowded into this modest one room apartment? Bernardo Soares, the bookkeeper; Alberto Caeiro, the shepherd; Ricardo Reis, the classicist; and Álvaro de Campos, a world traveler and man of leisure. Campos was the one who declared that Pessoa, too, "strictly speaking" did not exist.

"Same to you, fella'!" Pessoa might have retorted. He'd be reluctant, perhaps, but he does what I tell him. Can't help himself. Besides, how can a man who "strictly speaking" does not exist take umbrage? Take some of the umbrage, querido amigo, and perhaps a little humble pie? (And for dessert, sour grapes…)

I digress. Or do I? Is it not the case that *babouinisme* and *bouffonnerie* are hiding places as convenient as any number of heteronyms? *Babouinisme* can be a clown suit to disguise a painful truth. *Vesti la Giubba*, Leoncavallo wrote for his heartbroken clown. (The next act in the circus would have been a lion riding a horse, enacting the composer's name.)

Think of the worst, most unbearable moments of your life. Your wife tells you she wants a divorce. Your headmaster expels you from school. You couldn't stand to be there, so you retreated, changing rôles from actor to narrator and fleeing to the grammar of the sentences you give yourself to think. I am not sufficiently original to be the only one who resorts to this. Everyone does. Or at least some do. The intelligent ones, probably more than the others, but no one talks about it, the flight itself being a display of cowardice and shame.

These are the kinds of things you don't even tell your shrink.

Now what's curious is that in order to notice this phenomenon, there has to be a *you* behind the voice-over narrator. There's the actor, the narrator, and yet a third being concealed behind the first two. You wanted to disappear, but now there are three of you, and as the saying goes, "Three's a crowd." (Three can also be an orgy. Or a good age to be. Or the signal for the firing squad to pull their triggers.)

But perhaps the effort is to disappear by hiding in the crowd? Not what you had planned, maybe, but it can work. Better than you had expected. Or deserved.

Those old stylites who lived on the tops of pillars may simply have been trying to get away from the crowds of selves that were continually pestering them. That may or may not have worked, but it is probable that there were people clustering around them. Think about it! Imagine it. Smell it! There were no ladders by which they could have climbed down a couple of times a day to pee or move their bowels. Therefore, after only a few weeks, their pillars would have been entirely surrounded by a pile of rotting human excrement.

(Not really. Each of them would have had an attendant to bring them food and water, which from time to time they'd haul up in a bucket. A part of that attendant's job would have been to remove the accumulated ordure. It is not a problem that comes up often these days. But it was the fashion, or one might say the craze, back in the fifth century. There were actually four men called Simeon Stylites among whom we must disambiguate: Simeon, Simeon the Younger, Simeon III, and Simeon of Lesbos. There might have been still others, the more effective ones, on pillars so far from the madding crowd that they never attracted attention or made it into histories of the saints. They could have been like those French and Spanish kings all named Louis and Alfonso so they had to be numbered.)

[Nothing wrong with numbers, though. Romans and Italians used them as names—Primo, Secundus, Tertius, Quintus, Ottorino, Decius and such.]

{"Quintus IV *agricola est*"? Did that ever come up?}

Who are those pests intruding with their parenthetical questions and observations?

Would it be unprecedented (but honest) to acknowledge them as the heroes of our narrative? We could give them names, of course: Bernardo, Ricardo, Álvaro, and Cetera. They very well might prefer anonymity, though, and if they are our protagonists, their preferences should be respected. Common decency would require that—although I cannot think of a period in history where decency was common anywhere on earth.

Therefore, a retreat from the world. A search for respite in the study, in the text, and then in hiding places within the text. I have seen in museums recreations of scholars' studies, temples to tranquility and order, with the elegant carved and fanatically polished desks daring the scholars to do any work at them. Work is messy and does not comport well with such beauty and order. Who would dare demean the furniture and the chamber? The overwhelming temptation would be just to sit there, pretending to think long, long thoughts.

You have never read Long-long's thoughts? They are hard to find because he never wrote them down, so the book does not quite exist. He just sat there, for months, for years perhaps, with his writing brush his hand, impressively gowned and with a Confucian expression on his long, long face. Tranquility, prosperity, and posterity are what he probably pondered. What else is there to think about? Mortality? But that endangers the saintly facial expression and can cause wrinkles to appear (Heaven forfend!) on the forehead.

Heaven forfends but God forbids. Why is that?

TWO

I ought to explain to those who have never picked up *O Assassina-
to de Roger Ackroyd* from a news kiosk in some railroad station in
Vigo or Brada to read on the train that the narrator is the murder-
er. A lovely trick, although no one can use it anymore. How clever
of the noble Agatha! And yet, we realize later on that Ackroyd has
been less than candid with us. He has been feigning innocence—
because he had to. If the first sentence were "I did it!" there would
not be much mystery or any point in reading further. So the mur-
derer is relatively real but the narrator is an impostor. (Unless, of
course, that declaration turns out to be untrue and, after the narrator recounts the crime, an inspector of some sort enters to question some of the details that do not make sense. It then transpires
that Ackroyd is protecting someone else, whom he loves and who
really did it.)

[Or better yet, every character in the mystery confesses to having done it, so that it is the inspector's job to find the true confession {a good title} among the false ones. But this would be *Murder
on the Orient Express.*]

(And for just a soupçon of reality, we could have the pleasant, patient inspector fail, so at the end of the book the reader has
no idea who killed Vic Teem. Hard to sell, but that is evidence of
deficiencies in the aggregation of villains, thieves, and fools that
calls themselves the literary marketplace. In the real world, many
murders go unsolved. For all we know, most do. And some that the
police gave up on years ago, suddenly solve themselves, perhaps by
the confession of a dying prisoner, or the accidental exhumation of

a corpse by a farmer digging a ditch… To emulate that, we could reveal the solution in a passing remark in another book.)

Back! The putative narrator shoos them away. In their running shoos, they retreat on fleet feet, taken aback but in no way abashed.

Seeing a thing requires stepping back from it. Understanding a thing requires stepping back even further, and perhaps stopping the flow of time. Both of these are distortions, departures from the elusive truths we rarely glimpse and never understand. The writer tries to hide in that blurry welter. And insofar as he succeeds, he disappears.

Into that wardrobe, perhaps? Instead of a closet, there is a large wardrobe with a suitcase on top of it. (We shall get to that later.) Or into the bathroom? We may not have mentioned a bathroom, but we did not mean to deprive Bernardo of one. There is a tub with those iron feet and the porcelain discolored around the drain. He could lie in that. He could even fill it with water and write while bathing, as apparently Winston Churchill did. Many, many books.

(Mene, Mene, Tekel, Upharsin.)

[A Babylonian law firm.]

Excuse us, Mr. Donne. Or I suppose it should be Dean Donne (he was Dean of St. Paul's), but every man is an island. And every man and woman knows this. What could be lonelier than jostling through a life in which love and friendship never seem to last and whatever sense of purpose you started out with blurs and extinguishes itself? Meanwhile, you never have to send to know for whom the bell tolls, because if you can hear it, you can relax: it's got to be for somebody else.

(And better him than you, right?)

He's messing with us. Or more likely, he's just doing what cler-ics do, showing off to us with paradoxes and puzzles. If he'd said, "You're all alone in life and are going to die alone," that wouldn't have been news. Or memorable.

(But it wouldn't have been wrong.)

The phrase is famous not so much because the poet used it but because Hemingway recycled it. We accept it without thinking about it much. But if we scrutinize it even briefly, we can watch it disintegrate. And the more we look, the shreddier it gets. From what we know of Hemingway, is it likely that he sat around reading Donne's sermons by the light of a kerosene lamp on one of those safaris? Would we bet on him or on Maxwell Perkins, the bookish guy back in the office at Scribner's, as the fellow who came up with a list of titles from which Papa could choose?

From Bernardo's residence to his office is only a couple of blocks along Rua dos Douradores, but the journey is more extensive than it might appear. It goes from letters to numbers, from the literary to the arithmetical. Numbers do not have connotations. They say what they mean and they mean what they say. / Two, four, six. Hooray!

Higher mathematics can wriggle on the page and confuse you with imaginary numbers, irrational numbers, algebraic formula-tions, and the like. But arithmetic is clear: seven only means seven, unless you're shooting craps. And thirteen is a floor number hote-liers try to hide. Triskaidekaphobia, or the fear of Triscuits.

The notional room appears to be empty. But in notional rooms, appearances are the only reality. So it would really be empty if there were a "really." Soares is there of course but only reluctantly. One of the advantages of having someplace to go every day to do his work is that the room without him is purposeless, static, and inanimate. It doesn't even exist so that any human presence would be a distraction from the vacancy of its pure self.

He can sit at his table, of course and, by immersing himself in the making of sentences, obliterate everything behind him—bed, bookcase, and wardrobe. And the upholstered chair in which he sometimes sits and reads. But he is conscious of the table and the wooden chair, so that their Platonic idea is sullied. There are times, though, when the room is crowded so that it seems as though he is entertaining. Along with Fernando, there are Alberto, Álvaro, Ricardo, and a number of others only some of whom have names. There is A. A. Cross, who isn't quite a writer but does compete in puzzle and word game competitions in English newspapers. There are António Mora, a theologian; the Chevalier de Pas, who does not publish but corresponds with Pessoa; I. I. Crosse, the critic who occasionally reviews the work of Reis and Campos, mostly praising them; Vicente Guedes, who, like Pessoa. is an assistant bookkeeper who writes poetry, stories, translations, and daybook entries, and used to live in what is now Bernardo's apartment; Jean Seul de Méluret, who is, as one may assume from the name, French; and many others, whom Pessoa never got around to naming or who have eluded the research of scholars (as every single one of them would have liked to do).

They are a heterogeneous crew. Some were prolific but some published very little. Or nothing. Maria José, the only female in the group, is a tubercular hunchback who never published but wrote a long, impassioned letter to a metalworker who passed under her window every day. And she never mailed the letter but instead held it to her bosom as if it were from him to her.

How many others were there? As many as we like.

Now imagine that the angel passes and they all fall silent at the same moment. Listen to the vertiginous emptiness, realizing that this is what they, too, are experiencing. Writers try to convey the quality of an event, but in this instance, the reproduction of the event in the minds of readers is magical, although the magic is fragile. The slightest sigh can ruin it, shattering each individual consciousness so that we are as we were before.

Nothing, in all its majesty and mystery! It would be difficult to keep one's attention focused on it, but there are occasional interruptions of sound to remind us of the majesty of silence. Bernardo's pen, an old-fashioned one that takes steel nibs, scratches briefly now and then. (I know I gave him a Pelikan a while ago but Bernardo likes to amuse himself sometimes by seeing how many words he can get from a dip of the quill pen.) [In Yiddish, a *kvellpen*, although it sounds like quill pen, is a fountain pen because it *kvells*, or fills up. And a quill pen is a *feder* (feather).]

There is no sound when Bernardo is thinking. With the Pelikan he can write in something approaching absolute silence. But the steel nib of the quill pen occasionally catches on the grain of the paper, especially on the upstrokes. The noise is negligible and does not call attention to itself but rather refreshes the emptiness of before and after.

Or he can be sitting in a chair, reading, and that makes almost no sound at all except for the occasional whisper when he turns a page.

Paradoxically, if it's too quiet, you can't hear the silence. The racket of your breathing and your pumping heart provide a blanket of white noise within which silence lurks, so you have to imagine it. And, harder, you have to believe it.

Am I getting carried away? I do hope so. Anyway that is the aim or at least the hope. One way of not being here is, obviously, to be somewhere else. And when the sentences are going well enough to have a momentum, there is the illusion that something is happening. Illusions are also somewhere else, plain or fanciful. Ill lusions, delusions. Salazar governed an illusory Portugal, and then persuaded the population to go along with him. Humor him, as they say. A dry humor, these people have. (People in Arizona in July explain that it's "a dry heat," which means it would be wrong of you to complain.)

During the intervals of silence Bernardo is perhaps thinking of the right word. Or he may be experiencing a moment of doubt about the entire project. No matter how good a work may be, if we go over it line by line, we are likely to find a place that could be improved. The best poem or novel or play is in actuality the least bad, and the author might have been better advised to sit in the chair with the pen poised in midair but without ever letting it descend to the paper. (After he had finished a draft of *Madame Bovary*, Flaubert fiddled with it for ten years!)

Writers should not be so intimidated and depressed. The perfect should not be the enemy of the good, but more often than not, at least among idealists, it is. [The trouble with the perfect is that it tends to be smug and condescending, which means that it isn't so perfect after all.] {So perfect? "Perfect," an absolute, doesn't compare!} It is an abstraction, though, and only exists as an idea. Heaven, I suppose, is a dream of perfection, an aspiration. If there were a heaven, it would assuredly be disappointing. We would find ourselves yearning for the mediocrities we left behind us, the assurances of a gritty reality in which we can trust. It takes nerve to reject ideals, and yet they can be paralyzing. And it takes wisdom to realize that the pretty-good is almost always better than perfection.

The road to hell is paved with aspirations.

That suitcase on top of Bernardo's wardrobe once belonged to Vicente Guedes and when he disappeared he left it behind. Bernardo has never opened it. He keeps it for the previous tenant, should he ever return to claim it. This is decreasingly likely but for Bernardo to dispose of it would be to admit that he has been foolish in holding onto it all these years. Still, his instincts as a bookkeeper are to take things as they are, neither improving nor worsening them, but merely entering them in a hypothetical ledger. More simply, he tries not to intrude. So it's still up there out of the way gathering dust. Bernardo has all but forgotten it.

So why should we take any notice of it? First of all, why not? But we are free to suppose that it may hold some of the possessions of Guedes, who wrote at this very table. The first part of *Livro do desassossego* is Guedes's work. (His style is slightly different from that of Soares, or so some Lusitanian Studies scholars have persuaded themselves.) Or of course it could simply be the case that Guedes also assumed a nom de plume and became Soares. Simply? As Captain Ahab used to say, "You are pulling my leg." Nothing about Pessoa is simple! [Pulling my leg = *puxando minha perna*.]

Puxe is the first word you have to learn in Portuguese. It is pronounced "push" and means "pull," and until you master it you will never get out of Lisbon's Humberto Delgado Airport.

Apparently Vicente and Bernardo were not sufficient for Pessoa's elaborate purposes. In any event, he was not content with these but felt a need for other voices, more remote from his own. More of a stretch. The challenge would have been to remain within his own tessitura while maintaining the illusion of otherness. Such poets would have had to be similar and yet distinctively different from Fernando. And then from one another.

One of these was Ricardo Reis, a classicist, who was a kindred spirit. He was the kind of fellow Pessoa might have encountered now and then in a congenial café. They would probably not have been friends but they could have been amicable acquaintances. Surely, each would have been aware of the other's work. (How many poets could there have been in Lisbon at any given moment? Twenty? Ten?) [For that matter, how many readers of poetry could there be in Lisbon, then or now? Or in all Portugal?]

Senhor Reis is plump and shiny-pated. But the jowls are what one notices first. They make him look authoritative, aggressive, and even angry. Imagine a district commander of the *Guarda Nacional Republicana*, a person of enormous power locally but a disappointed man who knows that this is the dead end of his career. This is as unfortunate for his criminals and suspects as it is for him. His deep conviction is that he should never be the most uncomfortable person in the room (office, cell, or interrogation chamber), and there have been few moments when he has not achieved this intention.

Reis, however, is a gentle soul, not at all like that curmudgeonly *coronel*. He is soft spoken. (Students find this trait menacing until they get to know him.) His special field of study is the use of particles in Greek. This is an area in which he has very little competition (in Portugal, none), which may be why he was drawn to it. (Or why Pessoa drew him to it.) Also, it is laborious work, requiring thousands of slips of paper that lead to such conclusions as: "The use of δ' ἀλλά is strictly circumscribed. It is always followed by an imperative, expressed or understood: and it is nearly always preceded by σύ." Not exciting, maybe, but reassuring. And verifiable. Impressive. That sentence alone would have taken months of meticulous research to verify. Poems are ethereal and only exist if the poet believes in them. He can never be entirely sure that he isn't deluding himself about what he is doing. But a grammatical rule has an actuality that is undeniable even at one's worst moments. In English, we would write or say "but," but there would be no way to suggest the range of emotion and emphasis the Greek offers. The heart of poetry is nuance, for which Ricardo could aim but with varying degrees of confidence that he had achieved exactly what he'd wanted. In Greek grammar there is less uncertainty.

It is perfectly plausible that Reis could have been sitting at a table at *A Brasileira*, say, at the very moment that Fernando and another of his heteronyms were greeting each other, but Ricardo, across the room with a newspaper before his face would not have been inclined to look up at either of them or to speak. Not that he is aloof or rude. He is shy—which can resemble aloofness. In silence, too, it is difficult to achieve nuance.

Young men and women sometimes imagine themselves as having attained, or inherited, lofty positions in society. They are generals, judges, cabinet ministers, or members of the peerage for whom special salutations are required when one addresses them or writes to them. This kind of fantasy has less to do with ambition than with a desire for an identity, as if rank and title provided answers to the uncertainties of that kind. (In his splendid ceremonial robes, a grandee may still be wondering who he is and whether he is truly entitled to these honors or is not *au fond* an impostor.)

Over time, the daydream changes, darkens, and takes on a vague sadness.

I am, in my recurrent fantasies, a person whose family estates have been lost, the ancient tapestries have been sold, and the manor house has fallen into such disrepair that the roof leaks. We lack the money and the enterprise to repair and restore the handsome building and now are like anyone else except that we have fallen from our accustomed altitude back into ordinariness, and this lack of distinction is our fault, our fault, our own grievous fault. We are now like all the other anonymous figures we pass in the streets, except that we feel a chagrin few of them share or would understand.

There is a cure, though, if we are willing to change our orientation. It isn't that we have fallen from our former grace but that we have traveled a good way on the road toward Buddhist obscurity. Rather than having to worry lest other people find out that we used to be important personages, we can learn to relax in the protective cocoon of the commonplace. Obscurity to the point of invisibility beckons, but only to those who are spiritually ready to appreciate it.

Alberto Caeiro has found his own road toward non-being. Or path, one should say. Passing as a shepherd, his status as a published poet is a joke. (Or is it the other way around?) At any rate, he is able to lie on hypothetical grass keeping an eye on his fictive flock and not worrying about his identity. His best-known work is a collection of faux naïf poems called *The Keeper of Sheep*. He is unusual among shepherds in that he carries engraved business cards that give his name and also announce his pastoral occupation. (He keeps them in a handsome, a black case, made of course of sheepskin.)

There was a real Alberto Caeiro, but he died in 1915 of tuberculosis, at which time Pessoa took up his pen (and name) and continued to write poems for him for the next fifteen years. Caeiro was then promoted to (or demoted from) reality. He claimed to be a shepherd and began to put that down on various forms that demand that one specify an occupation.

This shepherd business began as a joke, but he liked it so well and repeated it often and it became first a part of his repertory and then a guise, or disguise. He had become that pastoral figure who in theory leans on a crook and spouts simplified wisdom. "Wherever you go, there you are." It is either profound or moronic. (Can it be both?) [One of the strengths of Buddhism is that it is impossible to parody.] {Aren't all religions?}

He affects simplicity as businessmen affect sincerity. His is the *boue* for which we sometimes have moments of *nostalgie.* Too much of it can be tiresome, but now and again, in moments of fatigue, it bubbles up like cool, clear spring water to quench our desiccated and therefore thirsty spirits. Alberto finds this pleasing.

The Lord is our shepherd, but then, at a certain point, shepherds kill their sheep for their meat and their skins. The smarter sheep (are there any?) may suspect this but still their instinct tells them that the shepherd's knife is preferable to the wolf's teeth. Quicker and less messy.

When he is in the mood, Alberto sometimes expands on this conceit, claiming that he is accustomed to sleeping on straw in rude cabins—cahoots, they are called. Or outdoors directly under the skies. (If the rain in Spain falls mainly in the plain, it must do so, too, in Portugal.)

Gauguin tried this kind of rustification among the Tahitians, but it apparently failed to resolve his identity problems. In one of his paintings he asked, "Where did we come from? Where are we going?" In Tahitian? Both profound and moronic, as the pastoral mode requires.

Alberto is a figment of Pessoa's imagination, who is, by now, a figment of mine. It is all done with mirrors. But they can enable angles of vision otherwise unobtainable and unimaginable.

Do you know anything about Saint Eberhard of Luzy? (I dare say not.) Born into the Italian nobility, he gave up his dukedom to become a shepherd in Luzy, Haute-Marne, France. He wanted solitude and to live in prayer. This is a guy who must have read Vergil at an early and impressionable age and took him literally. The whole idea of the Eclogues is that they are a conceit. Vergil's figures weren't real shepherds and farmers any more than John Wayne was a real cowboy. But Eberhard believed the words he was translating, and his tutor, a mischievous friar, thought this was amusing and did not correct him.

So was Eberhard a real shepherd or only pretending?

Alberto is not a real shepherd either. Bernardo, Pessoa, and I understand this, and he probably does, too.

In order to avoid confusion (or the necessity of much rereading) I have imagined that these heteronyms mostly understand one another. And to an extent, they do. But they understand the world in different ways. All those students at their desks in aisles and rows of a classroom, listen to the teacher and watch as she writes, in fiendishly neat Palmer script, some bit of information. That for example Hobart is the capital of Tasmania. Well, it's true, but it will be true for these boys and girls in different ways. Some with think of Tasmanian devils and wonder exactly what they are. (Carnivorous marsupials the size of a small dog that are now found only in Tasmania.) Others will wonder whether the Hobart scale company was formed there. And one may think of a grade-school friend named Hobart Fischer and wonder if his parents knew about Tasmania and were oddly fond of it. (Was Hobart conceived there? Does it have imports and exports or is it entirely self-sufficient, like Tolstoy's estate in Yasnaya Polyana?) [This is a bright kid, apparently.]

And so it is with Alberto, whose sheep would have been imaginary even if he had been real, as opposed to St. Eberhard's ovines that were real but merely props in his fantasy.

If anyone had ever challenged him as a faker, Alberto would have been delighted and flattered.

One advantage of heteronyms is that if you submit a poem to some magazine and they reject it, the rejection is not yours. It has your address, of course, but editors are inattentive enough never to wonder why so many poets live in the same building on the Rua dos Douradores. It would be unlikely, because poets dislike one another more often than not.

But would avoidance of rejection have been Pessoa's motive? Just as likely, it could have been a distaste for the opposite result. Suppose that the editor of *Wooden Chicken* or *Parataxis* likes one of your poems and wants not only to publish it but invites you to submit more in order to make an impressive group. I can't help thinking that Fernando was likely to have been more leery of success than he was of failure. He would not have wanted to be "known," even on the paltry scale that poetry journals offer.

I remember that W. H. Auden disliked identifying himself as a poet. When asked by hearty salesmen in bar cars on railroads what his "line" was, he replied that he was a medieval historian, which foreclosed on any further conversation. In the same way, Pessoa might have wanted to avoid encounters in *A Brasileira*, in which people, even a very few, might come up to congratulate him on the poems they had recently read and to inquire (as these people all too often do) whether he wrote with a pen or on a typewriter. (Why do they want to know? Do they suppose that if only they used the proper instrument, they, too, could be *littérateurs*?) [And that could make their lives more interesting?]

Pessoa is too polite (or too unassuming) to answer with what frequently pops into his head—that he writes with his brain. It is true but unhelpful.

It wasn't absolutely necessary for Pessoa to name each wraith he summoned up from the dark matter and into the light of day. This one was a friend and that a mere factotum. (*Largo al factotum della citta./ Largo! La la la la la la LA!*) Or he might choose one, a virtual stranger, to be his listener.

You are alone and you sigh at some memory that has arisen to color your moment's mood. To whom is the sigh addressed? It implies a hearer, even if not distinctively imagined (let alone named). He is one of the gentlemen of the bedchamber, a sympathetic presence of limited powers but he does understand you. He sympathizes. It is not his fault that he is a projection of yours. He certainly need not apologize. (To you?)

Is he a single being or is there a whole staff of factota? (Not a word in dictionaries, but it would seem to be the logical plural, wouldn't it?) My guess is that one is sufficient. A fac-totum by definition does everything. (But he could have an assistant, maybe.)

A bit baroque, no? Álvaro de Campos is not convinced. He understands nihilism, of course, and even subscribes to it, but he does not take it seriously. (Cancel my subscription!) There is very little that he takes seriously, as if to do so would be a lapse in manners. (But how does he know what Bernardo is writing or thinking? Have I not explained this? Anyway, one of the advantages of being a figment is that most of them are on good terms with one another. It would be chaos if they were to argue among themselves. Family quarrels, like civil wars, are more savage than disputes between strangers.)

The smile on Álvaro's face is both condescending and philosophical. He realizes, as Bernardo perhaps might not, that originality is likely to be wrong. And even if correct, if absolutely brilliant, it is different from the usual view and therefore is likely to attract ridicule or outright hostility. If you have a truly original idea, it is wise and certainly safer to keep it to yourself.

Campos has been sitting at a sidewalk table of a bar in the Zona Rosa, thinking about zero, which is not nothing. It is, in fact, a powerful number, because if you multiply any number by it the result is itself and if you divide any number by it, you get infinity. Meanwhile, in addition or subtraction it is shy and does not affect the sum or the difference.

He puts his glass down on the table and, even though it is a stem glass, the bartender has chilled it so that it leaves a faint circle of condensation. Which looks like a zero. A circle that somebody long ago had figured out could stand for nothing. (Inventing it or discovering it? As someone invented or discovered infinity and assigned the lemniscate to it. Were these quantities always there, like Brazil? Or did they not exist at all until the mathematicians voyaged to their shores?)

It was an Indian, I think, who designated the circle as a symbol of nothing, but wherever he came from he was like a Zen master, truly devoted to nothing, setting it as a goal, and adopting it as a fundamental principle of his life. Of all life. The sequence of prime numbers is increasingly strenuous to determine, but zero declares itself at once, even to the simplest child. From two cookies take away two cookies, and what do you have left? Zero cookies! Which may be nourishing to the mind but not the body.

And perhaps tears.

Zero is a difficult or even impossible goal to realize. To get to zero degrees Celsius, or a perfect vacuum, or a physical motion that has zero resistance and therefore could go on forever… These are impossible dreams. Nature taunts us with our dreams. That is part of her allure.

It is difficult to imagine nothing, but there is a way of sidling up to it. Think of the prime number beyond the largest prime number that has been discovered. It must exist, mustn't it? But until some-one has found it, it doesn't. All there is is an ache, a need for it, a longing. (Do mathematicians long? Except of course in division.) Or take the next digit of pi—that is, the one beyond the last one that anyone has bothered to calculate. Same ache. Same vague sense of neediness.

Nothing is like that.

And as an extra benefit, if someone were to pass by and be so rude as to ask Álvaro in the course of conversation what he was just thinking about, he could reply in truth, "Nothing." (Such an en-counter has never taken place, but then it didn't have to. Existence is nothing to boast about.)

Álvaro is not the kind of man who argues. He gives orders (in a quiet voice and with a smile) and asks questions, but he is not interested in facts or even, for the most part, viewpoints. Still, if a question is put to him that he finds interesting, he may deign to participate in a discussion.

When there is nothing to discuss, one may discuss nothing. Its history, for instance. The Sufis are so focused on God that they deny the reality of everything else. Or, *bref*, they acknowledge nothing but God. (Nothing *and* God?) Álvaro is brave enough to take the next logical step so that he believes in nothing. Including God. He is a nihilist more or less. (Less? Does he, as a nihilist, believe in less than nothing?) And yet he will refer us to some of the Sufist ideas, which were (are?) intriguing. Various Sufi masters have declared that no one can acquire his wisdom by studying and reading books. It can come only through experience. ("Annihilation without ritual!" "It is easy to repent but harder to repent of the repentance.") It must sprout in the novice's heart and begin to grow. He will at first think it to be a weed and try to pluck it out. (O Lord, Thou pluckest…) Only if he fails in this attempt can he proceed on the path toward dark enlightenment as the plant thrives, flourishes, and, at length, brings forth its beautiful blossom—which is God.

Álvaro takes a sip of his coffee and puts his tiny, translucent, fluted cup back on the indented zero on its tiny, fluted saucer. "Even so," he says, more because he is pleased with the trope than to convince anyone, "the blossom must eventually go to seed. That is what blossoms are for, no? And if one chews these small, bitter seeds, one may begin to see the true darkness that is behind all light."

He raises an eyebrow slightly but enough for us to notice (now that it has been pointed out) and then looks away to signal that the discussion is over.

I don't understand it (nobody does, not even the physicists who proposed it) but there is dark matter in the universe. Indeed, there is more dark matter than the kind we are aware of and assume is real. There are black holes, which I don't understand either. Bathtub drains, say, with existence itself whirling about and then disappearing along with the tub.

Have the philosophers neglected to take these holes into account? They discuss the impossibility of the existence of nothing. To exist, there must be a thing. Things, by their nature, exist. (Those who maintain that some things don't exist are called "noneists." [How do you pronounce that? "Nun-ists?"]) Nothings, by their nature, don't exist. The argument goes something like that. I am simplifying, but it is a simple, even a simplistic idea, and I do not misrepresent it by declaring it in non-obscure language. There can be ideas of unicorns or the present king of France, but the whole point of such constructs is that they have no being. They are not. (The grammar gets a bit giddy here, but that is always interesting to watch.)

Pessoa took a different, even an opposite view. Things that have being and that you can see do not exist. They are ephemeral wisps and will go away. Fantasies are perdurable. Fictions are immortal. That is why the gods are immortal. If they existed they would die.

Quine (Willard Van Orman Quine) holds that "some things do not exist" is a self-refuting proposition, implying that some things are not things. Is this a plausible academic view or merely a soothing mantra?

Many eastern sages recommend mindfulness as a way of getting through the trials and vicissitudes of life. Álvaro knows better. The difficult state to attain is mindlessness, in which a person can merge entirely into the surround. Drugs and alcohol offer modest tastes of that contented selflessness. Go into your garden and pick up a small, smooth stone. Hold it in your hand. And try to be as insensible of it as it is of you. It desires nothing, fears nothing, knows nothing, and believes nothing.

And any stone can tell you this, if you think of asking it the question, so it doesn't matter which one you pick up. (Avoid gemstones; they sometimes have an attitude and presume to sparkle, which can be distracting.)

What am I trying to accomplish with this writing? To hide, of course, but also to demonstrate to myself that I am more than a bucket of sensations. I am aware of these but I can only be aware of myself by inference and indirection. And these are never sufficient. They can be tempting, like theology, but I have a nagging hunch that, like theology, they are elaborate inventions of people with too little to do.

Are they wicked? Or practical jokers? I don't think so. I assume that in order to exchange heavy labor out in the hot sun for a seat on a high stool in some cool scriptorium, they have to pretend to believe. Pretenses are tricky and difficult to maintain because over time they are either constraining or they turn real. And let us say an Amen, which is neither devout nor sarcastic but terrified.

So, who's left? As many as you like. Scholars have identified at least 136 of these fictional alter egos, and there may be more. If you are hiding behind a *nom de plume*, the *nom* may also want to hide— and the undiscovered ones would therefore be the most successful. Beyond the man who never was is the man who is not even suspected of having been. The unknown unknowns, as Secretary Rumsfeld called them—and he could grapple with ideas, having been a wrestler at Princeton.

Dei sub numine viget.

THREE

I am not alone in sensing a dwindling from what used to be. Declension, degradation, diminution. Certainly my Portuguese countrymen feel whatever it is unless they have become so accustomed to it that they are no longer aware of it. Take Brazil. (They did!) We used to own it. We had an empire. And then we didn't. What happened to it? You can't simply misplace Brazil. You can't apply the usual methods of wondering when you last used it. What were you wearing? Check your pockets, yet again.

Say that you lose a penknife or some similar trinket. In a little while, you stop looking for it and even forget about it, but the slight unease continues, for months, even years, until you lose that, too. Brazil remains a sore spot.

Who is speaking? We have not indicated a heteronym. Perhaps it is Pessoa, himself. He is of course unaware that someone who was born the year he died is putting thoughts in his head. But if he were, would it make a difference? Thoughts have to come from somewhere, don't they? Thus they are never truly ours but more like library books we have checked out but will eventually have to return. (Are there fines for overdue thoughts?)

I am doing to him no more than what he did to Alberto Caeiro, taking up his pen and, finding that there was still ink in it, continuing his work. Years before, when Sir Philip Sidney died, his sister, Mary, Countess of Pembroke completed his translation of the psalms. (But did she publish it as her own work? Or her brother's? Neither! She never published it at all. To publish is, by its name and nature, vulgar. Still, anyone who was anybody in England read it in manuscript.)

We can perhaps concede that thoughts must come from somewhere, but if there is a Svengali manipulating our minds, he is so clever at it that we are seldom aware of him and therefore do not suspect him.

Thus the high value we ascribe to our individual identities may be illusory as well as arrogant. The ancient Greeks were not only more modest but also more accurate when they invoked the muse for whom the poet believed himself a mere amanuensis. "Sing, Goddess" is not just a formula but an acknowledgement that the poet has had help from elsewhere.

"Elsewhere" is Pessoa's natural habitat.

To assemble all these figures in Bernardo's small apartment is a conceit. A heteronymous bash. It never happened, but why not let it? The past is frozen, like ice and the future is gaseous like steam. The present is liquid like water and we can swim in it, fish in it. And drown in it, I suppose. At any rate, its fluidity makes it possible for us to imagine what we like (or fear) and even realize some of these phantoms.

There is now a Restaurant Pessoa on the Rua dos Douradores, in which people can imagine the dead poet dropping in for a plate of *mariscos fritos*. They can even look around in the hope that Bernardo or Vicente may show up as they used to do, at least fictionally. It is a fictional restaurant but you can look it up on Travel Advisor. Apparently, they offer a Pessoa stew. (A possible name for this book? Or too cute?) I'd like to think that it is an empty bowl in which you can imagine whatever food you like.

Another world is what we are thinking about. And surely, we are allowed or even obliged to imagine better worlds than this, if only as a way to survive in this one.

Too grand? Probably, but let us consider the question in a smaller and more focused way. You get up in the morning and, in the kitchen, pour a handful of beans into the coffee grinder. A familiar enough task to be habitual. You don't have to think about what you are doing. And then, because you are not thinking, one of the beans misses the grinder, bounces off the tabletop, and falls to the floor. You have to decide whether or not to bend down and pick it up. Not really worth the effort, is it? And yet you hate to be wasteful. And messy. And it was your fault, wasn't it? So you bend down and with your thumb and forefinger, seize the bean and put it with the others in the grinder.

So? So you cannot help imagining that this cunning and brave bean managed somehow to escape, or at least to postpone for a few seconds its doom. A few seconds only, but what is time to a coffee bean? This enterprising specimen outmaneuvered you momentarily and it deserves credit. This is utterly absurd, and you know that, but in your mind you have already framed the absurdity and cannot expunge it. At most you can despise it and reject it (it was despisèd and rejected among beans) but it is now in the record as an alternative version of history. Who is to say with absolute confidence that inanimate objects do not have a will of their own? Or a destiny? [Nicolas Malebranche believed that each atom had its own destiny. Go ahead, look him up!] Which of us is so committed to the enlightenment as to insist that it cannot be wrong? The bean escaped. It was wanted. It was recaptured. And sent to the grinder with its companions. And you felt a tiny satisfaction when that happened, didn't you? (Relax. I am not going to try to do something about *Á la recherche des grains perdus*.)

We are too smart to believe in this animism but also too smart to believe absolutely in our unbelief. In the children's stories we read so many years ago, such an account would not be extraordinary. Fact vs. fiction; knowledge vs. faith; truth vs. myth. Valencia vs. Madrid Real. Who knows which side to bet on?

Outside the temple at Delphi, some Greek wag inscribed on one of the stones the famous words, "Know thyself." And we have fallen for it, or, worse, have missed the point of a good if subtle joke. Animals know themselves, of course, but they do so without thinking, which may be the only way to do it. Only mankind sets this as an exercise so that it is doomed to failure. If one is inquiring into the self, then there are necessarily two selves, the subject and the investigator. In other words, one who embarks on such a path is exiling himself from himself and therefore is two. Self-consciousness is what sets us apart from nature. This is what we got from the tree of knowledge and the reason we were ejected from Eden. Self-awareness was the apple of the tree.)

It is only the unexamined life that is worth living. Self-consciousness is the curse that God did not mention, perhaps because he knew, as the best practical jokers do, that we would eventually discover it on our own.

It is plausible that Gauguin's painting is a warning. The happy Tahitians have no idea who they are. They don't care. There are coconuts on the trees and fish in the sea. Why worry?

Pessoa's solution to this problem was to call into being enough selves so that the question could be referred to a committee for study. Isn't that what the connoisseurs of cunctation in academics and business generally do? The question in the message is not important. What counts is getting it from the In box to the Out box.

If it comes back, which may or may not happen, that will be time enough for the professional procrastinator to deal with it.

Or a better metaphor: think of a chorus, a very good one, well-rehearsed so that they are all together and on key. You cannot pick out any individual voice. The chorus seems to have its own voice unlike that of any of its members. A different, richer timbre. Most of the choristers are good singers but not quite good enough for solo work. (Or they may have jobs or child-care problems that limit the time they can devote to singing.) But what they discover is the joy of participating in this new thing, this collective richness, beyond the capabilities of anyone. Or any one.

Except Pessoa.

Who has been speaking? The general tenor sounds like that of Álvaro de Campos, but on the other hand, its prolixity argues against him. Campos doesn't like to go on too long, preferring epigrams and, on occasion, defiantly stupid puns. Both of these require less effort and less attention. What he might ask is: aside from Otello, are there a great many generals who are tenors? (Handel's Giulio Cesare was an alto castrato.)

If not he, then one of the nameless ones? An aristocrat of self-effacement.

Or, given his tastes, he could be a ghostwriter for Guedes or Soares, whispering into an ear in order to maintain his own anonymity. (Ah, no nimity, eh?) [Is that a nimiety?]

We should not get too exercised about this uncertainty. Behind whatever author may be credited, there stands Pessoa, and then, behind him, me.

The difficult part is saying all this without moving one's lips, so that the grotesque dummy seems to be speaking. Would it be at all comforting to think that the blather we hear every day from people on the streets in busses and trains, in offices and restaurants and almost everywhere is the production of unseen ventriloquists with a wicked sense of humor?

As ophthalmologists say, better or worse?

Time turns us all into heteronyms, or, more complicatedly, homonyms who are, nonetheless, different people. Marianne Moore, for example, evolved from year to year, and the older ones had the advantage in that they could revise what their predecessors had written. The author of a poem of a decade before was in effect dead, and her heiress could add, subtract, or revise whatever was on the desk.

To improve the old poems, of course, or that was the intention. The results varied.

The sixty-year-old Marianne could ruin something the forty-year-old version of herself had written. At forty, she was less experienced but perhaps livelier in her perceptions and associations.

And that, perhaps, is the point—that we hardly exist at all except as temporary versions of ourselves. What I was yesterday is similar to what I am today but not identical. Sometimes radically different. This must have been true with Fernandino also, but in his case that growth and change would also have been occurring in all his heteronymic companions.

Pessoa found this disturbing. And distasteful. His preference was for the stability of oblivion. Not death, but close to it. Think of a gas range and how you can turn the flame down so that it barely shows blue over the little holes in the burner. And a touch more, even. But the next touch extinguishes it. To keep the pot at an ideal slow simmer, you have to perform a delicate calibration, holding your breath as the flame holds its gassy breath, too.

There is a great difference between "I don't believe in anything" and "I believe in nothing." The first is mere failure; the second converts the failure into a triumph. (*Bandiera rosa trionfera!*) Nothing as a species of perfection, an intellectual and spiritual ideal, may be difficult to grasp, but difficulty is not a reliable indicator of truth or falsity. Pessoa left behind him trunks full of papers, writings of his perceptions and beliefs, observations, and reactions to the spectacle of existence—but he did not try (or want?) to publish any of this. One can understand publication as the transformation of nothing into something. And the something is always a compromise. Readers and even scholars will interpret (misinterpret) every word, analyzing and "appreciating" any text into a distressing caricature.

To be an adequate reader, you need more than intelligence and an honest soul. You must have the modesty to avoid expropriation. Think of Emily Dickinson's relative who took out all her delicious dashes. In the comfortable darkness of the trunks the words cannot be distorted or betrayed. Yes, I understand this, but candor requires me to say that I do not publish anymore because I can't. No editor wants to bet on me. (The result is the same but my reasons are less admirable.)

Race horses like running but if they understood pari-mutuel machines, they'd like it less. And they might refuse to run if anyone was watching.

Pessoa and Emily Dickinson, and who else? That's the beauty! We don't know! (We can imagine dozens, hundreds.) It was untoward that Fernando and Emily's wishes were frustrated by their disobedient heirs.

Pessoa went even further. He warned against finishing any book or even reading too many pages sequentially. The only explanation I can imagine for so drastic a regimen is that he yearned for the illiteracy he had lost, as if it were not the Tree of Knowledge that Adam and Eve should have avoided, but alphabets.

His thoughts rejected themselves.

And who is to say that he was wrong?

A quick method for self-assessment. You go to the greeting card aisle of a drugstore or supermarket and look about you. Happy Birthday, Happy Anniversary, Happy Everything, with cute puppy dogs and pussycats or homey scenes—some of them self-referential. What is the point of sending a Christmas card that shows a mantelpiece covered with greeting cards? Is it a suggestion for how to display these things? Is it merely a confirmation of the fact that, yes, this, too, is a card, confirming the others and confirmed by them?

Anyway, the self-assessment is fairly accurate. You can measure the levels of your taste and character by noting the number of minutes (or seconds) it took before you felt a wave of nausea. This is how people live! How they think (if, indeed, you call this thinking)! You feel distanced. There is something wrong either with you or all of them, the shoppers, the people who actually purchase these things. And realizing this, you have to ask yourself if you want to be one of those people. A dismaying question. The thought is disgusting.

You can calculate your degree of refinement by dividing your level of distress by the time it took you to feel it in your viscera.

We never admit this to others or even, sometimes, to ourselves. But secrets are often significant truths, which is why we repress them. And the darker the secrets, sagt Sigmund, the more significant the truths.

Not knowing how to write, the cave painters at Lascaux could not sign their work; they didn't feel the need to do so, perhaps thinking that the paintings were themselves sufficiently individuating. Or perhaps that individuation of any kind was irrelevant. Either of these conditions seems paradisiacal compared with the distasteful competitiveness of modern art and literature. Musicians do not choose anonymity—although they can find themselves at odd moments in blind auditions, playing behind a curtain so that their sex and their looks and gestures do not adulterate the performance or influence the jurors. Or the conductor.

The auditioners may not like it, but they will admit—albeit grudgingly—that there is a purity to the exercise.

But it can't last long. No impresario is going to book an auditorium and put up blank posters announcing NOBODY, in his/her DEBUT or FAREWELL PERFORMANCE. The critics would be nonplussed. And the audiences, affronted by being toyed with, would stay away in droves.

But are there deaf auditions? Losers often think so.

What are these fictive personages anyway? Hypotheses. Personifications. Metaphors. It is only when we consider them in such a light that we begin to understand their value. It might be clearer to refer to these men and women as metanyms, for if heteronyms are "other names," then "metanyms" extend farther and include both sides of the transformation, the self and the other, cohabiting amicably as they often do in actuality's blur.

That formulation would be closer to the commonsense understanding that Bernardo is and is not Fernando. They are alike but can be disambiguated. Which makes them a third thing in their bothness. Bothitude? Bothificense? Bothiosity? (All those and more.)

The question then is not why Pessoa invented all these semi-beings but rather why other writers (all other writers?) have not done so. It was not a Pessoan gesture but a human one. All those who lie in bed in the dark waiting for sleep fragment into a symposium of selves discussing the issues of the day and the eternal verities (or falsities), unless they are subhuman. Or superhuman. It is difficult to conceive of Moses or Jesus or Buddha or Mohammed having such a swarm of alter egos. They knew who they were.

Or thought they did.

Álvaro de Campos allows a flicker of a smile to appear on his face, raises his absinthe glass in the gesture of a toast, and says, "That is the first interesting thing you've said in the last several pages."

As the arboriculturist Senhor António Nussbaum observed in one of his papers, "The nut does not fall far from the tree." The apothegm provides an insight into Pessoa's work habits. He invented but he was happy to get whatever help he could from the ephemeral churning of the real world. Soares had a rented room? So, of course, did Pessoa—when he wasn't living with relatives. He made a meager living translating business correspondence into and out of Portuguese. (Only a few years later, Ettore Schmitz would study English in order to acquire sufficient fluency to manage the correspondence of the bank he worked for in Trieste. His "native English speaker" teacher at the Berlitz School was Giaccomo Joyce.

[Schmitz wrote *The Confessions of Zeno*, which he signed as Italo Svevo, his mother being Italian and his father Swedish.]

A menial job? But so was that of Senhor Suarez, the assistant bookkeeper (*escriturário assistente*).

Pessoa's attitude about obscurity was paradoxical. He claimed to desire it but he kept all his observations and comments in a series of trunks and boxes, and one must infer that he had no objection to posthumous success. Or even fame. I'd be surprised if that suitcase up on the wardrobe wasn't similarly stuffed with notes and jottings Vicente Guedes left behind in the same hopeless hope.

It is sublimely Pessoan. The teasing notion that experience is coherent and holds some kind of meaning turns out in the end to be just one more delusion and an indication that we have learned nothing from our many previous mistakes and humiliations. *Estúpido! Bobo! Babaca!*

Clouds. Soares writes about the difference between clouds observed in the city and in the country. He says the obvious things, albeit gracefully. My guess would be that their impact is enhanced in the countryside because the sky is larger or seems so without the tall buildings slicing one's view. But there they are, floating in the direction of the prevailing winds and making us feel small.

The question that arises in my mind is why Soares is holding the writing instrument (whichever we decide to put in his hand). Why not Pessoa himself? Or is it by this time habitual? Has it become an obligation so that he must think up things for Soares to write?

Poets are often on the alert for promptings, but there is a pushiness to their constant quest. They want to express themselves? They want to add to their body of work? These are unattractive reasons for defacing yet another blank page. But to do the same

thing for Bernardo is less self-centered, and Pessoa felt less embar-
rassment when he noticed that he was, again, wondering what to
do with the image, the metaphor, the thought that had popped into
his mind.

Pessoa was by no means a moron and could recognize what he
was up to. He was not fooled by these flimsy but habitual self-de-
ceptions. Until he was. And at that point he could invent another
alias with another biography to go with the new name. The Baron
of Teive was perhaps the last of these and was less than ideal for
Fernando's purposes. For one thing, because of the Baron's fears or
flightiness or mere impatience, he hardly ever finished anything. A
heteronym who can't write is a mannerist being. Useless, but then
many aristocrats are. He may have thought so, himself, because he
eventually committed suicide. But do not grieve for him. He was
imaginary, remember, and his death did not prevent Pessoa from
continuing to write for him.

Pessoa may have had suicidal thoughts (who doesn't?) but he
never acted on them. He died of TB, which was, at the time, a
fashionable disease. Chopin died of it, too, as did Chekhov, Balz-
ac, Molière, Alexander Pope, and hundreds and thousands of unknowns.

It is not inconceivable (it can't be: I have conceived of it!) that there
were some heteronymic figures, imaginary playmates really, who
were too fastidious even to begin anything. Who wrote nothing
whatever. These were such intimate companions that Pessoa didn't
have to name them. They were there, with him, ever-present as
some of your teachers are, reminding you of the difference between which and that, and so and as. They are perched on your
shoulder like pirates' parrots, iterating their grammatical cautions.
They used to be something of an annoyance but over the years you

have learned to tolerate them and even grown fond of them. They are yours, after all, and their intentions are probably good. They do not intrude with announcements like "Polly wants a cracker" or "Fuck the pope." (What kind of person would spend hours teaching his parrot to squawk such things? Are they intellectuals who want to claim that their avian chums have Gilles de la Tourette's syndrome?)

Álvaro is sufficiently amused to want to name the patient, whimsical bird trainer. Why not? Where is it written that heteronyms cannot have their own notional companions? Inasmuch as they are creations of Pessoa, it would be natural for them also to have aides, attendants, epigones, acolytes, and other such clones. Who might, in turn, have theirs. I know very little about self-replicating crystals, but their very existence is intimidating. Their molecules reproduce as if they were alive and they would, if left to themselves, fill the universe.

Into the diminishing space they have not yet appropriated, let us put these generations of fictive men and women, thoughts of thoughts, shadows of shadows. Pedro is the one with the parrot. He may not have an eye-patch or a cutlass but even in a business suit (especially in a business suit) he has a raffish look for which the green bird perched on his shoulder is only partially responsible. ("Fuck the Pope!" "Kiss my ass!")

Álvaro pauses for a moment to imagine a board meeting over which Pedro presides. Why do the others tolerate such absurd grossness? Perhaps he is the principal stockholder of the company, having inherited the shares from his father who was, as they say in business, a real pirate, although he did not sport an eye-patch either. The board members are well paid and have become accustomed to these occasional avian interruptions.

He signals to the waiter that he should bring another coffee. As he waits for it, Álvaro wonders if Fernando has any idea of Pedro's fictional, fractional (fractal) existence. If he did, would he be delighted or displeased?

Yesterday today was tomorrow; tomorrow today will be yesterday. Is it any wonder that our day-to-day lives are so repetitive?

Alberto Caeiro has been writing an essay on solitary confinement, which he concedes is cruel but maintains is interesting for its philosophical implications. At the merely practical level, it is a convenient way to punish men who are already in prison, but whether the wardens have realized this or not, it is merely a redundancy, a further constriction of their captivity. And its message is unmistakable—that we are all in solitary confinement and that solitude is our universal habitat. One can learn to enjoy it, as shepherds do. We do not simply lie about in bosky dells playing on our oaken flutes. We think, or at least some of us do. And we have plenty of time in which to consider the great questions. Is there, for instance an ethical implication of alone-ness?

When Immanuel Kant was "traveling widely in Konigsberg," he could amuse himself, looking into shop windows or inventing stories about some of his fellow pedestrians. Or wondering about whether any of them held their socks up with strings attached to their pockets, as he did. There is no reason to suppose that he experienced any degree of solitude.

But think: if you are the only living being on earth and everyone else (and everything else) is illusory, do you not feel the same limitations as do visitors to museums, who are warned not to sit on the chairs, which are furniture exhibits?

Real things can resist or even fight back. Imagined things are helpless and therefore demand more kindly and considerate treatment.

Arguendo, if fantasy beings can claim protection, shouldn't real ones deserve at least as much? (Assuming of course that there are real ones: there is always that possibility.)

Bernardo takes the speculation further: Solitude is freedom. The solitary man learns to live without other people and does not have to seek them out for money, love, or glory. His self-sufficiency is what compensates him for the tragedy of birth. Most men grow into a slavery of dependence, but he is not so constrained. His liberation is a foretaste of the freedom of death, where he will be beyond pain and pleasure, pride and shame, and all wants and needs. This is the condition of angels, or would be if there were angels.

The likelihood is that few prisoners discover this. Their limitations keep them from enjoying their obvious advantages. It is reported that some of them go mad, which is actually a sane and sensible thing to do. The dissolution of the self is the cell's open door through which they can walk at any time, leaving behind only a husk, an animal that eats, drinks, shits, pees, and sleeps. The poor beast is nothing to him just as he is nothing to it.

Bizarrely, the warden and the guards, by bringing him to the edge of the saintliness that hermits long for, have enriched him beyond their inadequate imaginings. They are like cows in the meadow that know nothing whatever of butter, cream, or cheese. The prisoner is also unaware of the benefits of his situation, at least at the beginning. Some grow into that knowledge, age like whiskey, wine, or certain cheeses, and only then liberate themselves.

Of course, I have never experienced this myself or had an opportunity to verify my theories. I do believe in them, but I am neither a criminal nor a lunatic. Or if I am, I have not yet been found out. I suppose I could arrange to interview a prisoner about to be sent into solitary confinement and then again after he is released to learn about his experience.

But that would only be anecdotal. To make my case, I should have to carry a clipboard and interview hundreds of such prisoners. Which would be strenuous and tedious. Worse it might ruin my elegant conceit. Given the choice, I'd opt for elegance rather than truth. (If we were to limit ourselves to the truth, I would not exist.)

One might devise an entertaining application of these views, Álvaro supposes. If we assume that the full range of human possibilities is available only to prisoners in solitary confinement, and if we could devise a way in which this information got out into the world, then we would have people clamoring to get into prisons. And to make room for them the criminal inmates would have to be released. Evicted. Inside, monastic contemplation and quiet; outside, the incoherent, unattractive hurly-burly of serendipity. The plot—if we deign to have one—might involve a prisoner who was discharged and who was curious about the great number of applicants contending for admission. The peripeteia would be his realization of what he had lost and his attempts (probably futile) to return to his old cell.

Its absurdity comes from the reasonableness of the donnée and the inevitability of the denouement.

It is almost worth Álvaro's while to jot this down or to tell someone. But not quite. As it so frequently happens, the thought is enough.

("Monastic" generally applies to orders of monks, but it could also refer to Leibnitz's monads. Odd, how few people are unsettled by this.)

What appears to be a well-turned-out gentleman enjoying a cup of coffee in the afternoon sunshine of a fine day is more complicated than one might suppose. As I have indicated earlier, some of these heteronymic personages have in turn created alter egos for themselves. Or deputies. We cannot be sure that this is the "real" (anyway primary) Álvaro de Campos or his figment—who is also named Álvaro de Campos. Practically speaking, it makes very little difference, but who is speaking practically? Álvaro—either one— has the kind of mischievous wit that would prompt him to think up another version of himself with the same name and have him sipping the black coffee at that café. Simply to deceive Fernando? Perhaps imitating him in his desire to escape notice.

Or as a joke? Why not? If their books are any good, many authors create characters that behave perversely or in ways that they did not intend or expect. (So it wouldn't be a stupid joke.)

The situation in all its complications is both theological and ridiculous. (But ridiculousness may be a hallmark of authenticity, especially in theology.)

It might be helpful to distinguish between Álvaro de Campos and Álvaro de Campos[2]–but helpful to whom? Surely not to Campos, but to readers? Perhaps. (But how many of them are there? Enough to spare the cities of the plain?) Anyway, why should their convenience or their irrational desire for clarity affect what we are about? If it is that important to them, let them write their own damned books. (The first few days are exhilarating, but tedium then sets in, usually before page 20.)

Pessoa dips his pen point into the inkwell before him but does not write. For whatever reason, the pen remains tantalizingly suspended over the ink well with the enceinte point holding its drop of ink hanging in the air, impending.

FOUR

AN ANTHOLOGY

STONE

It has atoms wiggling, electrons and protons
whirling around and spaces in between.
You should be able to put your finger through it,
or at least a needle. But no,
                    the stupid stone
refuses to understand and won't be persuaded.
                                    —Vicente Guedes

DICTATOR

"Suck it!" he says. His dick? His revolver? Which?
You're terrified, you're disgusted. Nevertheless,
you decide at once that the gun is probably cleaner.
                                    — Jean Seul de Méluret

GEOPOLITICS

America, Britain, China, Russia—
they are all crazy, planning for progress, working
on grandiose schemes to benefit mankind.
We Portuguese know better. Our hopelessness,
the font of our wisdom, keeps us safe.
                                    —Ricardo Reis

DAILY ROUND

In my room I stand at the center
and turn slowly to the left, and turn
further and again. The wardrobe rises
in the east and sets in the west, as does the bed
and the desk and the easy chair. And it was evening
and then it was morning: another dreary day.
—Alberto Caeiro

LANDSCAPES

The landscapes we have seen yesterday
or years ago return as dream landscapes.
Uninteresting then, even more so now.
—Bernardo Soares

TREES

Let us be as simple as trees:
God will love us and make us us
as trees are trees.
We can pray for nothing more.
If He gave us more, He would have to take it from us.
—Alberto Caiero

OX CART

If I were an ox cart
squeaking down the road,
and then at nightfall
moving back over the same road,
growing old, I would not wrinkle
nor would my hair go white.
When I was used up,

they would remove my wheels
and I would lie in a gully,
broken, on my side.

—Alberto Caiero

VERDADE

The only thing there is is the real world.
It is not us, just the world
that is not in us, and there the truth lies.

—Vicente Guedes

WINDOW

I sit with my head propped on my hands
with my elbows on the high windowsill,
sitting sideways on a chair after dinner.

—Bernardo Soares

PURGATORY

Nothing happens in Heaven.
Whatever goes on in Hell repeats and repeats
until even tortures grow boring.
But in Purgatory they strive,
repenting of sins and errors, cleansing themselves
of any last speck of identity,
so those who ascend at last to Paradise
are no longer themselves.

—António Mora

BIRD SONGS

The experts claim that some are love calls,
some are warnings of danger, and some

may have other meanings we have not guessed.
They cannot accept the idea of meaningless beauty,
although it is all around them all the time.

—Alexander Search

SUNDAY

Today is Thursday in the week that has no Sunday.
There will always be someone at the farms on Sundays.
To visit them is a pleasant excursion.
But for those who feel,
or even for those who think,
it is never Sunday.

—Ricardo Reis

METAPHYSICS

I have a bad cold
that alters the ways of the universe.
A cold turns us against life:
we sneeze our way into metaphysics.

—Álvaro de Campos

WEATHER REPORT

Give me blue skies and a shining sun.
Fog, rain, and darkness I have within me.
Anticipation? Sadness? Nothing at all?
From the moment I got up I was down.
The day turns to rain.

—Vicente Gueves

PRURITIS

What good are the theories
of one who feels his mind crumbling

like teeth in the comb of a beggar?
I fold up my notebook and scratch
soft gray scribbles on the back
of the envelope that I am.
Because it itches.

—Alexander Search

CREDO

I have no ideals, but nobody else has any.
Those who claim them are like me, but they lie.
In my imagination I love what is good,
but I lie to myself and know I am lying.
Like everyone else, I do not believe my beliefs
but until my death, I shall talk and read.
Account for myself? I am what everyone else is.
Change myself ? How would I do that?

—Vicente Guedes

MANIFESTO

All those things human beings attach to life,
what increase can they bring to my soul?
Only a desire for indifference
and the sweet indolence of the vanishing hour.

—Mário de Sá-Carniero

LOVE POEM

I do not want your love. It oppresses me
because it demands love back. I want to be free.
Hope is always the burden of affection.

—Manuel Leitão

WIND

Sometimes I hear the wind blowing
and find that merely to hear it and feel it
makes it worth having been born.

—C. Pacheco

IMAGE

I am sitting at the window.
Through panes the snow has blurred,
I see her lovely image, as she passes by…

Grief throws its veil over me.
I am less a creature in this world
than one more angel in the sky.

—Paolo Jardineiro

ENVIABILITY

The dishwasher, the old man who comes in to clean,
having put the chairs on the tables upside down at closing time,
the drunk who sleeps in the alley…
I envy them all because they are not me.

—João de Lebre

FIVE

What puzzles me, I am frank to say, is why Pessoa invented these many masks and then put whatever he wrote into an undifferentiating trunk in some closet. There should be a point to a joke, and there should be a victim into whose head the point penetrates.

I had a friend—dead now—who used to play games with poets whose work he disliked. (Or whom he disliked personally.) How on earth did a dope like that get hired by the English Department of Elite University? To satisfy the diversity requirement, perhaps? (If creative writing cannot be taught, then it doesn't matter who is pretending to teach it: your Milton scholar, on the other hand, ought at least to have read some Milton.) [It is politically incorrect even to think such a thing, but how do you prevent ideas from popping into your head, especially when reality prompts them?]

Anyhow, my friend would write a deliberately dreadful imitation of Doofus's poetry, exaggerating his/her style with its faults and habitual tricks. So far, no hurt, no foul. But then he'd type Doofus's name at the bottom of the page and send it to an obscure literary journal, to which Doofus was now far too well established ever to submit. And he'd put a stamped envelope in with the poem with Doofus's name and address on it. (These addresses are easy enough to find. *Poets and Writers* puts out an annual directory with this information.)

Okay? Okay? One of two things has to happen. Either the journal rejects the poem and mails it (back) to Doofus, ideally with a rejection slip. Or even better, the magazine, impressed by the name (the first and often the only thing poetry editors look at), publishes the poem and sends Doofus the three free copies that represent his/her payment. Either way, outrage. And yet, "What is to be done?" (Lenin's line, I think, or was he quoting Nikolai Chernyshevsky?)

In any event, none of this, however scurrilous, violates any law. And even if it did, how was Mr./Ms. Doofus to identify the culprit? So aside from being humiliated, Doofus is also made to feel powerless. He has won prizes and has such an inflated idea of his importance that he assumes there will be a time after his death when some scholar, putting together his *Complete Poems*, will turn up this deplorable graffito and include it, delighted to have been rewarded for his industry—or luck—in finding it.

If Pessoa wasn't making a joke? Then it wasn't funny but heart-breaking. Pessoa couldn't just pick up his stylo and write but had to hide from himself. In order to get in touch with his inner self, he had to disencumber himself of who he was. I can't remember which German *Dichter* it was (Schiller, maybe?) who could only write if there was the odd smell of the rotten apples he kept in his desk drawer. My guess is that the odor distracted him so he could pay to the poem the delicately oblique attention that writing requires. Pessoa, as Pessoa, was inhibited. Paralyzed. But as one of his heteros he could walk and sometimes fly. (Rilke, meanwhile, declared *Du mußt dein Leben ändern* [you must change your life], and perhaps Pessoa thought a change of name might help. Or be enough.)

We do know that Pessoa was an alcoholic and that he died in 1935 of cirrhosis of the liver. (Is there any other kind?) He was only 47 years old. What alcohol does is dull one's senses. Drunk, one becomes less and less a person (in Portuguese that would be a *pessoa*) and disappears at last into an undifferentiated soddenness.

This is close to the obliteration Fernando was seeking.

His heteronymic helpers were reliable assistants in that they could not abandon him. He had made them up after all. When he wanted them they were available and when he didn't require their presence they disappeared. Or, like servants in the old days, they turned their faces to the wall and pretended not to be there—while the nobleman whom they served pretended not to see them. (An elaborate transaction, really, requiring tact and the cooperation of both parties.)

More simply, they allowed him to cope with his self-consciousness. He didn't have to answer such questions as *Who do you think you are? Who cares what you say? Do you suppose that you have anything to add to literature's conversation?* Bernardo and Vicente and the others were not intimidated by such thoughts, which are depressing and mundane. (You cannot be mundane if you do not exist in the *monde*. So Fernando had to choose between being one of them or remaining silent. Not that silence is unappealing. But there is the evening to get through. And the week and the month. What is the purpose of a life of translating business letters and then having dinner and going to sleep? Day after day. And then you die. Why wait?

Nuts? But we all are. Those who write and those who don't. The non-writers may even be nuttier, because their way of getting through the deadening (literally) passage of time is often to resort to religion. Are Matthew, Mark, Luke, and John any less absurd than Alberto, Ricardo, Álvaro, and Vicente?

I do not dismiss these saints but I think it is fair to compare them to Pessoa's imagined companions, who actually did help him. You pray to Saint So-and-so to help you pass an examination, or get hired, or find your gloves. Do they come to your aid? Or minimally can you blame them if they fail to help you in any of these efforts? (But you don't—do you?—because that would be sacrilegious. And it would also require a deeper faith than you have.) The difficulty is that our existence is intolerable, and we survive by fleeing from it to alternate universes in which we feel less helpless and imagine that we have allies in our battles with adversity.

You are at a concert, at the Coliseu dos Recreios say, and the thought arises, absolutely unbidden, that the members of the chorus, every one of them, must feel at least from time to time, envy of the soloists. Sopranos, altos, tenors, and baritones... (Envy and maybe hatred.) What separates me from them? Are they really that much better? In the orchestra, which is very hierarchical, there are infinite gradations of jealousy and resentment. The second violins could perfectly well play the music on the stands of the first violins. And each player thinks now and then of his chances of moving up to the first chair when its occupant is killed in an automobile accident. (Or not necessarily killed: maimed would be enough.)

On the podium, with facial expressions that show his sensitivity and spiritual immersion into the piece they are performing, the conductor waves his baton to communicate speed, volume, and phrasing. Every member of the orchestra knows that he is a better musician with a far deeper understanding of the composer's intentions. Without question, he could do better.

In the audience, meanwhile, the men and women in the nosebleed seats look down at the richer patrons in the boxes and on the parterre. They have no quarrel with the people in those seats; their anger is directed against the world, or at least the unfair economic system in which some have more than they need while others are hungry. Or have to sit in the second balcony.

During a slow movement when the mind can wander, you can feel the ill will radiating everywhere. Even among the privileged on the orchestra floor where some seats are better than others. In the fifth through the tenth row, in the middle of the auditorium the view of the stage is better and the sound, too (although this isn't always the case; acoustics are unpredictable). Which means that the people too far in front or too far on the sides resent their more fortunate fellow-concertgoers. You then look back at the conductor and wonder if he knows what kind of hated and hating assembly of people is in the room, in front of him and behind him, too. Why not assume that he is well aware of all this and even revels in its scintillation? Perhaps he enjoys the vivid demonstration of the dangerously thin veneer of civility and culture over which he temporarily presides?

Is any of this true? Or is it just a manifestation of your mood (or mine)? How can we possibly know? There is no way to prove the truth or falsity of a perception. Or is it a thought, which is more likely to be trustworthy? It is a question you can only answer in terms of belief. How do you experience the world? (Do you have any control over that? Can you change it?)

You might as well have gone to a war movie, preferably with this music playing in the background as the corpses of men and horses pile up.

The brotherhood of mankind is a dream, and walking with your eyes shut is dangerous.

Why does Pessoa torment himself with such depressing musings? Not, I think, because he is trying to effectuate a cure, analyzing himself (it is possible: Freud did it—or thought he had done it), but because he has the conviction that by taking the most dismal view of things possible he may be able to see through the conventional hypocrisies to the uncomfortable truths of experience. It is the truth, the true truth that he is trying to discover and convey. Paradoxically, this means that when he writes a particularly painful passage, he is pleased with himself for his achievement. And for his courage, too, I dare say. Another reason perhaps for his notional associates and colleagues. He can avoid seeming proud. Dissociated from them, he can take pride in them.

Before we leave our houses or apartments (or rooms) in the morning and after we get out of bed, we get dressed. Of course we do. In most places in the civilized world, it is louche and even illegal to walk around naked. Therefore, we are obliged to put on what can be called a costume, which suggests theatricality. Nakedness is a kind of veracity no one wants to confront. (And most of us would not be comfortable either as exhibitionists or voyeurs.) Now, generalize only a little and we get to *Civilization and Its Discontents. Disfigurements. Distortions, dishonesties, distresses,* etc. Or to Pessoa. It is not a stretch to think of these alternative personalities as costumes. He could disguise himself simply by believing in them. Either with great force of will or practically none, he could let himself be changed to anything he wanted. Almost as if putting on a different tie. A sheepless shepherd, even. Why not?

He couldn't have been worried about his readers and what they thought. With the work in fragments in a series of trunks and cartons piled high in the curiously capacious closet of his room, there were no readers. Or editors. Nobody's backtalk. Or misinterpretations.

To a certain extent, every writer, as soon as he unscrews his pen cap, initiates an imposture. He is no longer himself but the voice arising from the words he is writing. The web is of the spider but the spider is not the web. He may try to keep close to what he thinks of as his real self but he is not at all obliged to do so. He can exploit his odd freedom by assuming traits and characteristics that are nothing like his own. To see how they feel. To see what that new timbre tells him of the world that he could not see. hear, taste, or feel on his own.

Or just to change from the guy who cleans up the cat vomit and takes out the garbage to the one who sits at a desk and writes. They aren't—can't be—the same person.

He is a man on a beach with an imaginary lifeguard up on the lookout platform with his nose covered in zinc oxide to prevent sunburn. The man on the beach takes off his sneakers and his watch, rolls them up in a towel, and goes in for a dip. A wave knocks him down and the lifeguard, although imaginary, saves him. It can happen. It has happened, again and again. *Credo quia absurdum.*

What did he want? And what did he really want? The cartons pose those questions, challenging us to put ourselves in Pessoa's place (haven't we been doing that?) and ask whether he hoped that his quixotic gesture might be nullified. Vergil directed that, on his death, the manuscript of the *Aeneid* should be burned. Most schoolboys have reason to regret that his clear instructions were ignored. But wasn't that his intention? He's got this epic poem that is probably snarkier than most readers suppose. Aeneas is something of a shit. Dido is a legitimate heroine and Turnus is a hero, but Aeneas? He is a pompous cad. What if Augustus were to decide that the poem was subversive? Offensive! *Lèse majesté!* (And less and less *majesté.*) The emperor could have all Vergil's work destroyed! He could erase all traces of the poet's existence. But if it were known that the poet had ordered that the work should be destroyed, that might cause Augustus to relent if only to annoy the poet. At least the *Eclogues* and the *Georgics* might escape destruction.

Probably the executor was informed that the decedent's instruction was to be ignored.

And Pessoa might have been playing such a game with Fate. Putting the pieces of paper into cartons is not at all the same as burning them. The opposite, even.

My guess is that he was of (at least) two minds. People who are not of two minds have less than one that is fully operational. Without an ability to maintain two different views (at least), there is no possibility of irony.

On a hazy day when the light is right you cannot tell where the sea ends and the sky begins. The sea-blue sky and the sky-blue sea are the same or so close that you cannot discern the line of demarcation. It is like that when you consider Alberto Caeiro, who was born in 1889 and died in 1915. Really. An actual person who was a writer. Pessoa liked his work so well though that he continued it, bringing the poet back to life as a heteronym. It was a game that became a habit.

Can you do that? Can you get away with it? Well, if you put all the posthumous poems in a trunk and nobody knows about them except perhaps a very few close friends, the chances of your being found out are quite small. And if you are caught? I know little about Portuguese copyright law. (There's a sentence I never expected to write!) I assume, however, that it prevents people from stealing work and publishing it as their own. What legislator could imagine somebody *adding* poems to the corpus of the corpse? This still would at worst be stealing the dead man's name. But what harm is done? You can always claim it was an *homage* or a parody.

(Both of those are allowed, I'd expect.) If the judge is a stickler, you'll get off with a warning—which in Portuguese will be *Aviso*.

If it isn't a crime, then I am not guilty. Or I am guilty but of something that isn't a crime and the sentence for which cannot be severe. At worst, what I'm doing here is resuscitating Fernando and all his minions and continuing his (their) work as he continued Caeiro's. If you sail out in a small boat to that invisible line a couple of miles out and just keep going, you rise into the sky where you can remain at least until darkness comes. After that it is ketch as ketch can.

The rules are different for painting. Picasso is dead, and it would be illegal to paint more Picassos, or to paint them and try to sell them as his. That would be fraud. Or just *homage*, if you don't try to sell them but only hang them on your walls. In that case, they are either copies or, more interesting, fictional paintings, in the style of Picasso and with his signature, but not his.

Poetry (except for the lyrics to pop songs) has almost no commercial value, so what Pessoa was doing (what I am doing) is untainted by greed—which has no place in the arts anyway. Except wait. If I were to forge a manuscript page of "The Wasteland," I would be flirting dangerously with the law and would be up there in the realm of real dollars. But the value wouldn't actually be in the poetry. Even if the page were real, its poetry would have been leached out of it and into everyone's head, so that now the piece of paper would be worth a lot but only as a souvenir. It would be like that pair of Napoleon's gloves in the museum in Milan. Or a signed baseball (unless the signature is counterfeit).

The better comparison would be with the knucklebone of St. Wenceslas (killed in 935 by his younger brother Boleslav, who is remembered as "Boleslav the Cruel.") The knucklebone is in a reliquary, probably in the Cathedral of St. Vitus in Prague and the belief is that Wenceslas's piety and virtue somehow still inhere in the small piece of tissue rather than in the memory of his charitable works. As Napoleon's courage—or foolhardiness—inheres in the gloves, or Eliot's talents in the piece of paper rather than in the words he set down.

Do they ever have dances in St. Vitus's Cathedral?

You don't see them so much anymore now that everybody has a phone that takes pictures (even pretty good ones), but there used to be artists in museums with easels and paintbrushes making copies of the paintings next to them. I think it was okay with the museum just as long as the copies were of a different size than the originals. But who is going to come into your living room, sit down, glance at the small landscape on your wall, and wonder if it is a Dou? (Vermeer would be difficult to bring off.) The guest whips out his tape measure and… Good grief! It is three centimeters larger than it should be? (Dou, you will remember, was one of the *fijnschilderij*.)

So the content is relatively worthless—the poem or the image. What makes the object costly is that the great man touched it and it is "authentic." It is a true fiction, not a mere fictional fiction. (Here's a howdy-dou!)

Did any of this worry Pessoa? Did it appeal to his innate impishness? Or nihilism? My guess would be that he wanted to put in a good word for stupidity. Aside from Dostoievsky's *The Idiot*, most of literature praises intellectual achievement and intelligence, but these have their limits and there is a case to be made for their absence. If men were smarter, they might from time to time suspect how dumb they are. And they might infer from that how modest they should be.

Writing assumes a reader, at least a notional one. Fernando (or is it Bernardo?) allows himself this indulgence and creates a deliberately sketchy and theoretical Other, whom he addresses and with whom he has an imaginary relationship. (Aren't all relationships imaginary?) He cozies up to Other, calling it/him/her "beloved." It is a dizzying idea: Other becomes a character. (Or it may be that Dizziness, too, is a character.) Pessoa confides in Other, confessing, for instance, to the "almost ecstatic pleasure of lying."

A lie is just another word for a fiction. A pejorative word perhaps, unless "pejorative" is also a lie. It is the comparative of "malus." The superlative is "pessimus," with which Pessoa seems also to have been quite familiar.

I can't help thinking that Pessoa loves Other for his/her/its ability to understand these things. Or anyway not to be much bothered by their inherent contradictions.

One way to resolve these metaphysical difficulties and distinguish between lies and fictions would be to go to the window, climb through it, and test the "reality" of the paving stones four stories below in the Rua dos Douradores. But if Bernardo tried such a thing, what he would discover is that the stones aren't real because he isn't real either. Death isn't real. Fictional characters, like Greek gods, are immortal. (Remember this, Ivan Ilyich! You can die repetitively but you keep popping back up and will through all eternity) A character can appear to die but only to inspire or intimidate us whenever their whims (or ours) prompt.

Is that not comforting, my beloved?

Now and then, it is pleasant to sit in my armchair as the daylight fades. There comes a time when it would be reasonable to turn the lights on. (They have come to expect it, I think.) But I can choose to sink in my room and in my chair into the ocean of gloom. When I am exhausted, I close my eyes, not to sleep necessarily but only to stop the barrage of images with their irrelevant and incoherent information. It is peaceful to let go of all that and float in a waking doze. The eyes are tired. But the ears, as if sensing an opportunity, take over and begin their random reporting. Sounds from outside continue to intrude like the rumble of carts over the cobblestones, the metallic complaints of trolley cars in the next street, an automobile horn, a boy passing the building whistling an annoying popular tune. Then the sounds, too, subside. Or rather they change in character, for after a certain point they come more from inside than out. There is the just barely perceptible but unmistakable noise of someone clearing a table to carry the dishes and flatware into a kitchen, and the flushing of a toilet. Occasionally there are digestive sounds from inside my own body that are happy to join in this impromptu *Konzertstück*.

Reality is muttering to itself, perhaps reassuring itself.

But why would it have doubts? Doubt is a manifestation of higher thought. Men and women have doubts. Cats and dogs do not, nor birds. They stroll or swoop from one moment to the next, content just to be. We are not so confident. Is this all? Am I missing something? Does any of this mean anything?

As with religious faith, such a degree of doubt is difficult to achieve and maintain. And as with religious faith, that kind of doubt holds out the promise of wisdom.

But in the end, even nihilism fails.

Here's a puzzler. Is Bernardo's Other the same as Álvaro's and Vicente's? Does each figment have his own figments? Or do they all share the same one?

I am of two minds about this, which seems only right and proper. The question is almost moot, though, because Other never says anything. She/he/it only listens. Or, like God, is merely imagined to be listening.

We may suppose that God used to listen. And what He heard made Him sick. He puked. The present universe is the vomitus of the one before. Indeed, there could have been a whole series of these wretched (and retched) creations. This is a cosmology no less plausible than any of the others but it has seldom been proposed. Is the sound of a toilet flushing in another apartment Other's comment? Or God's.

One of the most attractive traits of Other is her (*his/her/its/their* is just too cumbersome) namelessness. The other heteronyms have names and, indeed, are their names. But they may be like cats that do not deign to recognize their names, which are only for our convenience and the vet's records. Other disdains such self-indulgence. And she has a point. If the Pessoan desideratum is obscurity, namelessness is a step in the right direction. Nameless and faceless, she exists only sketchily, careful to leave no fingerprints, footprints, or DNA, more meticulous than even the best criminals, who often slip up so that the forensic teams find clues. (Luckily for us, Other is probably not a criminal.) We therefore have to take her on faith, which puts everything else we take on faith into some degree of doubt. As if non-being were contagious.

In the sweet, umbrous crepuscularity of my room, I sometimes feel anxiety without any particular reason. I try to imagine something that could prompt such uneasiness. I am emerging from a dark forest, heading for a seaport, but afraid that the ship has already left so that I am now alone, cut off from all friends and companions. I cannot blame them, though. It is my fault; I should have allowed myself more time. What else is there in the forest anyway but the passage of time that no clocks mark?

Out at sea, the lights of the vessel must be gleaming on the dark water, suggesting a happiness in which I could have shared if I hadn't been so disorganized. And feckless. Lacking altogether in feck. But there is no point in trying to reform. The ship has gone. *La nava va. La nava vavavoom.* And I have no idea when or whether there will be another sailing.

I always begin a piece of work against my better judgment. It is never an act of will but rather one of surrender. During the work, I cannot summon up the courage to quit. And when it is finished, it is not finished, because I know that it could be improved if only I had the patience. *A perseverança. A constância. A tenacidade.* It would only be with a demonstration of such virtues that I might discover whether or not I was any good. (But I fear what the answer would be. And that, too, is a sufficient reason for heteronymic hesitancy. Let them take the blame.) [That, too, is cowardly but at least is consistent. In the end, it becomes a fundamental principle.]

The things that are seen are temporal; the things that are not seen are eternal. Or imaginary. Or both.

The fire in the Cathedral of Notre Dame brought down the steeple, which, yes, is a shame. They will almost certainly restore it, but not exactly. Instead of the timber supports that burned, they are likely to use steel. Which means that they will not be restoring it but imitating it. The exterior will look the same, but the building—the structure—will be new. It has stood there on the Île for eight hundred years. But not exactly. They refurbished it in the nineteenth century century, changing it or, as they thought, improving it.

So it was six hundred years old and then it was two hundred years old. The spire dates back only to 1860 or so. Not to rebuild it, then, would be the architecturally correct thing to do.

It was Victor Hugo's novel of 1831 about the hunchback that popularized the church and prompted the renovations and eclipsed the stones and timbers so that the "real" edifice was in the novel, or at least the idea of itself.

There is anyway a perfectly good Cathedral of Notre Dame in Amiens, larger and to my tase rather more handsome.

Simply as an exercise in logic, let us equate the small pleasures in life—a good sleep, a good meal, an excellent cup of coffee, the timely arrival of a bus at the stop where we have been waiting for only a moment—with coins, which are also small. But we can feel them in our pockets and sometimes hear their comforting jingle. For larger quantities, there are paper bills, which are valuable only by general consent and a faith we all share. We plan our lives to accomplish the education of our children, the establishment of our reputations for trustworthiness and honest dealing, or the notional satisfaction of our own self-esteem. These, too, turn out to be valuable only by general consent—although if we were as honest as we claim, we would have to admit that such undertakings are abstractions, as unreal as the paper money we keep in our wallets.

There is an unimaginable chasm between the nothing that is not there and the nothing that is. We start with the first and then journey toward the second, and it takes a lifetime of unremitting effort. Intelligence is helpful but not, I think, essential. (Often, we learn that we must put it aside in order to keep it from beguiling us.) Far more important is honesty, the ability to look into the void and neither flinch nor deny what we have seen. We must resist the temptation to falsify it as we seek for comfort.

For the sake of honesty we must cling to despair—our only hope.

Very nice, but who wrote it? It is unsigned, which is fine with me, but it does prompt me to wonder what the use is of a pseudonym if you are going to write anonymously. (Were you lying then or are you lying now? Were you there then and are you here now?)

I am not being (altogether) frivolous. There are, after all, plausible uses for a costume no one can see. The writer didn't put it on for the sake of his audience but for his own good reasons. If he sits at his table and thinks of Reis, he feels his own identity fading away along with its constraints. He experiences the refreshment of being somebody else, Reis in this case. Distracted and expropriated, he can say things of which he might not have thought *in propria persona* and in ways that are different from his usual style.

It is not mere fancy then to imagine the unimpressive furnished room as crowded with Guedes, Soares, the other heteronyms, the Pessoas (Maria José as well as Fernando), and now me. (It is large and it contains multitudes—from the sampler by Wally Wit-man, or Wally Wally Infree.) For some of us the only way to explore ourselves is from time to time to be somebody else.

Have you ever imagined that in his glassed-in cubicle, your boss might be wearing a Superman costume under his business suit? (Sans cape, of course.) Does that help?

❀

Many of us had imaginary playmates when we were small. Four or five years old, maybe. Sometimes, there would be a doll or a stuffed animal that gave the playmate a corporeal presence, representing the companion the way idols can represent gods for believers. But we knew that the object was no more than a convention that we and the fantasy friend had agreed upon. I can't resist the thought that Pessoa's putative pen pals were a like phenomenon, grown-up but not much more sophisticated. Had he been asked, he'd probably have smiled and admitted that, yes, perhaps that might be the case. But nowhere, as far as I can tell, is there any reference to it in his poetry or prose. To set it down in ink on paper would have been to diminish, if not to destroy, the magic.

In our solitude we invent company. Indeed, when these imaginary companions are shared with other people, what we have is a cult. Or a religion, which we take seriously enough to kill and die for. Most of our history is a sorry story of wars between religions or even between sects of the same religion: Catholic and Protestant, or Sunni and Shia. Struggles of the forces of our imaginary friends against one another.

Yes, yes, we all know this, but how many of us are willing to look just a little further to the admission that these distinctions among fictive beings are the bonds that unite us or the disputes that divide us? Even if none of it is real. But then nothing else is real.

Joan Didion published a book about the death of her husband called *The Year of Magical Thinking*. I ask if there ever has been a year without magical thinking? Or a day or an hour?

❀

Two nights ago a gust of wind dislodged an earthenware flowerpot from a sill across the street. It fell to the stones below and of course shattered. Then the street cleaner dealt with it—the shards, the flowers, and the dirt in which the flowers had been planted. None of that is important except for the fact that the cleaner missed a clod of earth that, when it dried, resembled one of the cobblestones among which it had hidden. Its imposture was impressive, rather like that of chameleon that takes on the color of whatever is under it.

But that is not the point, either. What interested me was the brevity of the transformation. It was dirt and then a stone and then, as soon as someone stepped on it, dirt again. Of course. What else could we have expected?

My dreams have been like that—of impossible transformations, of miracles that are doomed always to destruction. Either I do not achieve what I was dreaming of or, worse, I do and find that I was mistaken. Whatever it was, it crumbled into worthless particles.

The metaphor, not particularly striking, is not my subject here. What impressed me was my recognition of its rightness and how it enacted on a tiny scale my vision of the world. The pot and the flower were vanities; the truth was in the clump of dirt and its disintegration. And even beyond that, I find it humbling to realize how much of what we see is the product not of our eyes alone but also our expectations. We filter out what we do not expect or are unable to grasp because our vision is not the same as our perceptions. A young man lying on a hillside and looking up at the stars has a vision of something less but also more than what an astronomer sees.

I close my eyes, which are nearly useless anyway, and contemplate these unyielding partialities to which I cannot respond except with a limitless sadness.

If the Iberian peninsula is the penis of Europe, Portugal must be the glans. No one ever mentions this. No one has to.

The meaning of Zeno's paradox has nothing to do with its mathematical guise. Of course it is true that before you get from A to B, you have to get halfway. And before you get to that midpoint, you have to get halfway there. The division keeps on infinitely and, if you are paying attention, you realize that you cannot move. So? The trick is that what paralyzes you is attention itself, which is the disease.

A long time ago, I wrote a line that is still in my head. Or part of it is. "Hope's the disease," it has hung in my mind for decades because it made a nicely abrupt ending for whatever the poem was saying. (I could try to find it, but that would involve the risk of coming across poems I no longer like, and what would be the point?) But I realize now that the locution was grievously flawed. There are varieties of hope, some of them toxic while others are relatively benign. If I were to say, "I hope it doesn't rain tomorrow," I am probably expressing a mere preference, and we are all entitled to our preferences. But if I am gambling on a horserace and I have figured out that a certain horse has a better chance than the other entries, I could say, "I hope it doesn't rain," meaning something rather different. The horse has not done well on a muddy track so now it is no longer a preference but a prayer, and the admission of prayers to my mental repertoire is an error. A prayer supposes that my expression of a preference can have an effect on the outcome, increasing the likelihood that, for example, it won't rain. With this kind of carelessness, we slip from the enlightenment all the way back to voodoo.

"Our thoughts and prayers are with the family," is what politicians inevitably say in response to a fatality of sufficient scale to capture the attention of the public. But thoughts are different from prayers and may even be their opposite. Prayers are intended to effect what happens in the world, while thoughts—intelligent thoughts anyway—make it clear that this is impossible.

How can we account for the fact that almost everyone, in moments of stress, will pray? Is everyone stupid? Or is there some other, less disgraceful and less implausible explanation? I suspect that the fundamental error we make is that we think of our lives as narratives. We have learned from reading too much that set-ups have pay-offs. Chekhov says that if there's a gun hanging above the mantelpiece, it has to be used to shoot someone by the end of the play. That's theater, that's fiction. It isn't real. What Chekhov should have said is that if there's a gun on the mantelpiece, it would be as likely as not that someone gets shot with a bow and arrow. Or hit by a bus. Expectations of coherence, then, are also wishes of a kind. Coherence and order are impressively absent from our real lives. We cannot let the transparent contrivances of authors and playwrights mislead us. When you read a book, it should not make you stupider. "Books are Keys to the Golden Doors of Knowledge," was written on a placard in my local library when I was a boy. It should have said that books are the keys to a lunatic asylum and they work only to let you in. They do not allow you to exit.

Intelligence, when it is under threat, hides. (It's the only intelligent thing to do.)

You can escape from this predicament, but to do so you must

tunnel your way out, as if from a penitentiary, using your finger-nails to scratch your way through the concrete of culture.

The truth would set you free, but for that to happen you have to be able to recognize it when it kicks you in the ass, even if it is not what you expected. Even if it is frightening and ugly.

Nothing comes of nothing. But everything does.

Many people can sound out the letters and pronounce the words. But that does them no good, because very few of them ever learn *how* to read.

I had taken a liberty—or so I thought. It seemed a good idea for these heteronymic henchmen to interact with one another, and I have allowed them to do so. But as it turns out, Pessoa did the same thing, although with more ambition and greater humor. Án-tonio Mora, for example, was a critic rather than a poet and he often reviewed the work of Caeiro and Reis, elucidating and praising them as bold neo-pagans. These essays may have been influenced by Mora's own predilections. He left fragments of various uncompleted works, among them *The Reformation of Paganism*. One can interpret this as evidence that Pessoa thought he was crazy. Or at least skewed a little, so that intelligent readers would not take his literary criticism too seriously. (He had a bee in his bonnet and perhaps a flea in his ear as well as a frog in his throat, all of whom could converse if I let them.) Mora's essays, however rich in random insights, were fundamentally odd—as if he needed treatment. It is more than likely that many of our contemporary men of letters might also benefit from therapy.

We may suppose, if we choose, that these three of Pessoa's *pessoas* got on but with occasional awkward moments. Figments rarely come to blows but they can insult one another. (Still, when a crisis seemed probable Pessoa could contrive to intervene and make peace. If he wanted to.)

His readers (there were never many of them) might be taken in, believing in the existence of the poets and the critic. Or if they were friends of friends, they might know what was going on and be amused at another level. In neither case was anyone harmed.

But if they had been? Would he not have continued to do exactly what he was doing? Readers, after all, are as much fictional beings as any characters in literature. They are, perhaps, the first and the prerequisite fiction.

Successes fade away; failures endure.

SIX

My life is not a catastrophe: it lacks that dignity. Worse than cata-strophic, it is boring. And I escape from it—or try to—in dreams and in these literary exercises, which are waking dreams. I recog-nize of course that this is a cowardly response, but what are my alternatives? Bravery and stoicism are so far beyond me that I can-not even imagine how it would feel were they my attributes.

Courage is what people need to confront danger, not shabbi-ness or shoddiness. To accommodate to mere messiness draws on qualities for which we do not have names. Indifference, maybe? Iterative blows upon the soul eventually have an effect, and one first becomes inured to disorder and then blind to it. Blindness is seldom proclaimed as one of the great human virtues, but my guess would be that it enables most people get through life. How else could they stand it? I have relied on it but am not proud of having done so. It is not admirable. The kindest view of it I can imagine is a degree of pity, but that would be for others. No one should bestow it on himself.

If the passers-by in the streets carry burdens of guilt for their deficiencies as great as mine, that does me no good. The denizens of hell do not experience any relief from their tortures simply be-cause they are part of a brotherhood of suffering. They do not con-sole one another. They are indifferent but they also know it would do no good.

Because I have no knowledge of the griefs and disappoint-ments of my fellow pedestrians, I can imagine that they are happy and healthy—if only to intensify my own feelings that waver between dissatisfaction and self-loathing. My desire for nullity is my only recourse. Nothingness has a purity that is the only possible anodyne for my banality.

Renunciation then? I can try, can even achieve a degree of it for a few moments, but the body's habits reassert themselves with their demands for air, food, water, and other necessities from the external world. So I have to renounce renunciation, too. (All its spiritual significance leaches out and I am left with a word game. Can I, for instance, renounce the renunciation of renunciation? It is grammatically possible but close to meaningless, which is why I like it.)

There are fundamentally two choices, no matter what the subject. We can prefer sameness or otherness. There is no reasoning involved. More likely than not it is a neurological disposition. And in either case our preference has no effect whatever on what happens. Sameness, however comfortable, becomes boring. Otherness—novelty, vicissitude, serendipity—confuses and exhausts us. Is this still me? What in all these giddy transformations remains constant (for in order for me to exist, something identifiable must persist)?

There is no answer. Or both answers are correct. What interests me about this inescapable paradox is … its sadness. The intellectual and emotional homelessness of each of us, from moment to moment, is heartbreaking. We are like that donkey that starves to death between the two stacks of hay of the same size at the same distance.

Or we would be if we were slightly more intelligent.

Brooks babble. Trees sigh in the breezes. Winds howl. But of course they do no such things. These conventional misinterpretations arise from our loneliness. We know better but we repress our knowledge, consciously and willfully. How much more of our experience do we distort this way? It is difficult to say because there are some (many?) stories we tell ourselves that are so convincing that we never question them.

Loneliness? More than that, it is our fears that prompt us to try to tame the wildness around us. We may understand what causes thunder and lightning, but confronting their intimidating power, we try to rationalize them (even in irrational ways). They are signs of Zeus's anger and somehow our fault. We are being punished, and that thought is comforting because if we could only figure out what we have done and behave better, we might avoid such harsh treatment in the future.

We know better. But we don't know better.

The idea of possession is necessarily secondary to our idea of the self, for unless there is an owner, there can be no ownership. My relation to the external world is that of a window-shopper, admiring objects in a vitrine perhaps, but without the intention of buying anything. What could I afford? And where would I keep it?

Or better, I see the world as I see landscapes. I cannot possess them and they are in any case useless. And fleeting, for they change hour by hour as the light changes and fades. What this teaches me is challenging: how to admire even while letting go.

These truths are obvious but painful. Most people prefer comfort, affirmation, optimism, and belief. What they want is happiness, which is elusive and temporary. Or fictive. They understand this but lie to themselves, because the lies are anesthetic. The pain doesn't go away entirely but it diminishes so that it is bearable. Almost.

Was that Soares? The paragraphs are unsigned, but that should not be surprising. Who signs paragraphs? You write a paragraph and then go on to the next. But there may be special circumstances like this one where a collective seems to be employed in the production of a text. Wouldn't the contributors in that case sign the paragraphs? Or at least initial them?

Not if they were working under pseudonyms. Then the only place to hide would be anonymity.

But suppose that against all odds Pessoa becomes fashionable, almost popular. (He'd have hated the academic vogue he now endures.) Scholars come and sort through the papers, envelopes, and café napkins in the trunks. They try to arrange these chronologically. Or assign them to the various supposititious authors. Guedes? Soares? Difficult to tell them apart unless they are handwritten. Typed manuscripts look much the same, except that Guedes's machine had a misalignment of the keys so that e and y were higher—only slightly—than the other letters in the line. If this is so, then there is a mechanical difference, which is far more reliable than mere judgment. (Mere? When it comes down to these subtle, delicate questions, the scholars have no confidence in their literary judgment and prefer evidence of the alignment of letters. And if that is true, then what was the point of all their years of study, all that work in libraries, and all those classes with only now and then a bright, interesting student worth their investment of time and effort? [And not every year!] Did it amount in the end to anything more than a pile of *merda de babuíno*.)?

Of course it is unlikely, but so is Pessoa's present vogue. (Few universities have Portuguese departments. There are a small number of departments of Spanish—and—Portuguese and a few more of romance languages with Portuguese 101 offered only every other year. So Pessoa gets taught, if at all, by the comparative literature faculty, who are Jakes of all trades but masters of none. And he has to compete with obscure Estonian dramatists [are there any who are not obscure?] or Greenlandic poets.)

But take it as a given. With a grain of salt. Or to the bank. For what it's worth. Or on faith. Or leave it.

Surely it is a possibility, however remote, that one of these heteros might have had the same thought, Despite the fact that it is a far-fetched notion. Or because of that. Anyway, Campos thought of it, and then thought it would be amusing to take a few of Guedes's cleverer squibs and copy them out in his own handwriting. And to be more subtle and mischievous, he leaves both copies in the trunk. Let them figure that out! Which one was the author's and which was the copyist's? Or plagiarist's? Or prankster's? (Only the cleverer ones would consider that last category.) *Por que não?*

Improbable. Which means that not even an imp would believe it. For one thing, imaginary people do not have distinguishable handwriting. Theirs were identical, and exactly the same as Pessoa's. (But that would have made the game easier for them to play, wouldn't it? And harder for the scholars.) We get carried away, as of course we were hoping to be. Any *away* is likely to be better than here. Or at least different.

When I was a small boy, old enough to read but not old enough to know anything, I saw that most department stores had an area devoted to Notions. It wasn't a word that suggested buttons, needles, thread, thimbles and other such sewing paraphernalia. I took it to mean what it said, and supposed that people who couldn't think of anything (or anything interesting or amusing) came there to shop for ideas. I was not clear about how these transactions worked, but there were a vast number of things I encountered that made no sense to me. Confident that these patches of fog would lift, I rather liked the suspense of not knowing. No longer so confident, I am mostly annoyed that the world keeps presenting me with new stuff to figure out. Salsify is okay, but what is machalepi? And what is amchur powder? (It is made from sliced, unripe sun-dried mangoes and is used in Northern India as a souring agent.)

We got carried away. Again. *Desculpe*!

Even alone everyone pretends. Especially alone.

It isn't something we talk about with one another and yet the shameful and self-indulgent fantasy of living forever or anyway as long as our books are on the shelves of libraries has crossed most writers' minds. The difficult idea of death, of absolute extinction, prompts us to imagine some exception by which at least a part of us may survive. Maybe the best part. And the law allows this. There are royalties, pitiful pittances that come in for a while after you die. I have received checks for sums less than the cost of the postage. I don't think they were meant as insults. The machines had taken over, cut the check, and put it in the envelope with no malevolence or snide intent. But say that I've been dead for a decade and a tiny check shows up for my grandson to cash. The $0.27 isn't so important as the fact of the transaction. My ghost [are there ghosts?] will be pleased. In the thirtieth year, though, whatever I have written will fall into the public domain; the checks will stop;

and I shall be as forgotten as my dry-cleaner or my butcher, toward whom I now feel a pang of sadness—that will pass in seconds.

Yes, of course I know this, but as we also know, facts don't matter. We can think whatever we like. Our liking makes it true or anyway persuasive. The question is whether Pessoa's pessimism was thorough enough to prevent such nonsensical ideas from growing in his mind like weeds on the side of the road. (The mowers come by now and then, but the plants are not discouraged and grow back—in a matter of minutes.)

But back to Fernando. It is possible that he was squeezing the nettle. I can't avoid it that I am going to die. But I can perhaps escape that dismal dwindling. Soares can go that way and Caiero, but that will have nothing to do with me. I sit here breathing and with my heart pumping but I scarcely exist. My imaginary collaborators, even gauzier than I am, are used to flickering into reality like fireflies and then fading back into the dark. That is their talent, as important as their literary work. Their existence is already compromised. They live in a virtual reality. (What virtue does reality have?) They have nothing to lose because death, for them, is a joke.

Or, on second thought, I may have it backwards. I was assuming (it is difficult not to) that Pessoa had a fear or at least a dislike of death. But as we read through his poems and his prose, we see that it is, for him, an enviable state. The nothingness we fear and to which he aspires is everywhere around us. *Ubique est.* We don't have to achieve it. All we need is patience and it will come to us. Assuredly and inevitably. If we appreciate this charnel house in which we find ourselves, we can understand his longing to extricate himself from the squalor, torpor, and sordor that surrounded him so that as he looked down at the Rua dos Douradores what he saw was the ruins of a conquered city, buildings with walls missing and scrawny wild dogs roaming the neighborhood in a desperate search for food. It seemed like an ordinary street in Lisbon, but he knew better. The transformation was coming, he knew, in which the necropolis would expand to occupy the entire city from which the terrified citizens had been fleeing for years.

He didn't worry about being remembered. Who would be left to remember him? For that matter, who would remember how to read? His fictive confederates were right not to care. And he could learn from them, a novice among an assembly of masters.

Stare at the sun long enough and you will of course go blind. But does it not follow that if you peer into the blackness of an open grave long enough you will see?

Perhaps the real question all along has been this: where did that last idea come from? It was there, all along, one could argue, lurking in the previous paragraphs, the obvious contrary waiting to be considered. But that's not quite how it happened. It popped into my mind. (Not Crackled, not Snapped, but Popped. As into Karl Popper's mind.) Or to put it a bit more mystically but also closer to the truth, it arrived from somewhere. From someone. And if I chose to call that someone Ferruccio (a name I've always liked from the first time I heard Tagliavini sing, because it was exotic and sounded like *farouche*), what horse is to say me neigh? The name has nothing at all to do with being sullen or shy but comes from the Latin for *iron*. But as soon as our little guy has a name, he acquires a minimal, shadowy existence that over time may seem more and more substantial. Not fleshed out, because no flesh is involved. And never solid enough to cast a shadow, but a bit less unreal.

Busoni's name was Ferruccio. And Lamborghini's. (He started out with tractors but then turned his attention to racing cars.)

It's Italian, but that could happen. If his mother was Italian and his father was Portuguese, a Ferruccio could be in Lisbon as easily as anywhere else. Let's give him a last name. Silva, maybe. There's a Silva on the Conselho de Ministros, in charge of culture. (Does Portugal need such a minister?) Ferruccio refused to follow the plan his father had laid out for his life and would not apply to law school; out of defiance as much as anything else he became a poet.

These people are like strings you dangle in boiling simple syrup: the sugar collects on them as rock candy. You think up a name and the biographical details appear like those sugar crystals. In theory, Pessoa didn't write the poems but he did have to write the biographies—a pleasant enough chore without any particular expectations. A game, really. The elder Silva was sent to work in the Portuguese Embassy in Rome where he met Serafina. Amor at first sight. And Ferruccio emerged into the world and was soon ready to take the dictation of Salazar.

He and Fernando met in a café, where he heard the thin, bespectacled man speaking about the Portuguese national anthem, which he was claiming, combined too much braggadocio with too much fawning:

> Hoist the undefeated flag,
> In the lively light of your sky!
> May Europe cry out to the whole Earth:
> Portugal has not perished.

What is the song asserting? That Portugal may have been defeated but its flag never was and you can even see it in the darkness? If you have to cry out that "Portugal" has not perished, you are conceding that the correction needs to be made to the prevailing view. It is nothing less than pathetic.

Hearing these sensible words, Ferruccio was heartened enough to introduce himself to Senhor Pessoa and that very day went to work for him.

The Polish national anthem is even more hangdog. "All hope is not yet utterly lost for the Polish people!" is its first line.

That meeting in the café? Never happened. Ferruccio wasn't Pessoa's hetero but mine. You were here while I was inventing him. To see what it feels like. It is mildly exhilarating.

Pragmatism doesn't work either.

Never say: "Never say 'Never.'"

SEVEN

A SELECTION OF POEMS BY FERRUCCIO SILVA

32
My sadness is subdued
because it is natural and just.
It is what should be in my soul.
My hands pick flowers
my soul does not see.

39
I have neither ambitions nor desires.
Being a poet is not my ambition,
but a way of being alone.

44
This afternoon a thunderstorm
poured down from the sky onto the hillsides
like a huge pile of gravel...
Like someone shaking a tablecloth out of a high window,
with all the scraps falling together
making noise when they land.

54
Walking the roads
looking right and left
and sometimes behind,

what I see every second
is something I have never seen before
with the essential astonishment
a child would have if it could really see.
I feel myself being born in each moment.

59

When you are in sunlight and shut your eyes,
you forget what the sun is
and think of things full of heat.
But you open your eyes, there is the sun again
and you cannot think about anything anymore,
because the sun's light is brighter than thoughts.

67

If God wanted me to believe in him,
surely he would come to talk with me,
knock on my door,
and say, "Here I am!"

70

He is a lovely, natural, smiling child.
He wipes his nose on his right arm,
splashes around in puddles,
collects flowers, loves them, and forgets about them.
He steals fruit from orchards
and runs away yelling and crying from dogs
that menace him.
Everybody thinks he's funny.
He scampers around the girls
who walk in groups along the roads
with jugs on their heads
and he lifts up their skirts.

He has taught me how to look at things.
He shows me everything there is in flowers.
He shows me how stones are pleasing
when you hold them in your hand
and look at them for a while.

In the late afternoon, tired from his pranks and follies
the Boy Jesus falls asleep in my arms
and I carry him home in my arms.

74
That lady has a piano.
It is grand but it cannot make
the music of running rivers
or the murmuring of trees in a breeze.

Who needs a piano?
It is better to have ears
and listen to Nature.

93
The hallmark of Swiss cheese
is its holes.
And with us, there are vacancies,
omissions, absences of thought and feeling
of which we should learn not to be ashamed.

EIGHT

One summer, home from college, my son-in-law worked selling Bibles in backcountry Alabama (which is most of it). This was, and is, Bible-belt country, but you'd be surprised how many families lack a copy of the Good Book. When the parents die, I suppose it usually passes on to the eldest child. This leaves the other eleven without a text to consult either for edification, or prayer, or consolation. If they simply need to pick a name, they can always consult their sibling's copy (but not take it out of his house). He also might allow them to use it for bibliomancy, which is closing your eyes, spinning around, then opening the Scriptures to a random page, which they believe will be prophetic. Tarot, actually, but without the need for a deck of cards.

My son-in-law didn't want an indoor job. But his resumé was mostly aspirational. He had been promised work helping a shingler on large jobs but these didn't come along very often. So "what to do in the meantime?" as the kulak yelled at Lenin who was preaching revolution. Lenin was stumped but my son-in-law-to-be got himself that gig, selling Bibles on commission. Now and then, someone would buy one, closing the door lest he see where she kept her coin jar. She would reappear with thirty-five dollars in singles, quarters, and dimes. My son-in-law said "Bless you," as if she had sneezed and then returned rapidly to the car for another book for the next house half a mile down the road.

He was doing all right, no worse than the other salesmen, but he knew he was smarter than they were and ought to be doing better. So he put his mind to the problem and, the next time he encountered resistance, he tried his new closer and claimed that this copy of the Bible had been autographed by Jesus Christ.

Stunned silence. The poor lady in calico asked him if he was being (breath) "sacrilegious."

"No ma'am," he'd say, adding, "and if you took it as sacrilege, I am truly sorry and I apologize. Of course I signed it, but the signature is not my fist. I've never written letters that were that pretty. It's as if I am in a trance. It's someone else's writing. And who else's can it have been?"

It shouldn't have worked (it didn't always) but my son-in-law has such an open, honest face and an expression somewhere between sincere and simple, that his prospects were dazzled enough to admit the possibility. (Even if he'd forged the signature, they would still be getting the Bible—its leatherette cover generously stamped in faux gold.)

"Didn't they wonder how Jesus had learned Roman letters?" I asked.

"Some of them may have figured that out, but by that time I'd be two farms away." (Big grin.) "And you are smarter than they were."

You see the relevance. My son-in-law's motive in telling me this hadn't been malicious. What he found remarkable was not so much his outrageous claim as the innocence of the wives in back-country Alabama. (The husbands were usually out in the fields.) Even if these farmers were wrong, they had faith and lived in a simpler world we would all long for if we didn't understand that their certainty was an illusion. We know better but are no happier for that.

Let me assert, then, with my son-in-law's persuasiveness, that my pen (or keyboard) wrote Silva's poems. In the style of Pessoa and expressing views similar to his. But as he told his customers, it was not my fist.

Nor was it Pessoa's fist in the works of Guedes and Soares and the others. For all we know he, too, could have been in a trance.

For that matter, we all could be sometimes. Or most of the time. It would be soothing to think so. The advantage of nightmares is that there is always a chance that you may wake up.

But am I making the absurd claim that while I am writing this, Pessoa may also be writing it? Or at least collaborating? Always be suspicious of Frenchmen in berets. Those are what collaborators generally wore. And because the French are thrifty, some of those berets may have been passed down from the wardrobes and bureaus of the actual collabos who turned in their neighbors to the Gestapo. Were these miserable antisemites or did they only want to buy their fields cheap? (Which is worse?)

But there are other kinds of collaborators. Think George and Ira Gershwin, Richard Rogers and Lorenz Hart, or Sam and Bella Spewack. (They wrote the book for *Kiss Me Kate*.) These collaborations bonded in pairs so that they became another unit altogether. So with Fernando and me. I could not write any of this without him and he, being dead, can't write anything without me.

Too grandiose? Grandiosity, when it fails, only provokes laughter. Let me declare, without pomposity, that I have no idea where this is going. I rely on him. Or them, if I count the passel of invented pseudos and heteros. (Did you have any idea that "passel" is a variant form of "parcel"?)

More simply, more directly, I can formulate the situation in Pessoa's own words. "Sometimes, when I wake up at night," he says, "I feel invisible hands weaving my destiny." Okay? You see? Those hands could be mine. He thinks his "real life" is banal and contemptible. That idea is true but was premature. The banality and contemptibility that so distressed him are also mine. And he is allergic to me as some unfortunates are allergic to cats. (Cat dander, actually, but what difference does it make?)

I have been assuming that Fernando approves of this relationship and, indeed, this project. But I have no reason to do so. He may be merely tolerating it. He may even resent my intrusion, my presumption. It is hard to guess. I know so little about the Portuguese worldview. Are there intellectual histories of Portugal? Are there studies of Portuguese humor? There are attitudes that are distinctively French, or English, or Italian. (Think of Jean Gabin, Robert Morely, or Marcello Mastroiani.) But Portuguese? What do they think about while they sit on the beach, repairing their nets? (Have you ever heard of Nicolau Bryner, the Portuguese Gabin, more or less?)

For my purposes, I have supposed an amicable relationship. But even friends quarrel. Sometimes they can put their differences behind them, but not always. They are only human. (The Portuguese are a subset of humans, no?) I need him, and my guess would be that people like being needed. But my understanding of o espírito Português is sketchy at best. In an out-of-the way country that is in effect a suburb of Europe (as are the Balkans) the Portuguese might well be particularly touchy and all the more proud because they have lost their empire and have little left to be proud of.

But wait, wait! They have thirty-seven Olympic medals. And two Nobel Prizes. (One of them went to António Egas Moniz for the invention of the prefrontal lobotomy; José Saramago won the other.)

It could be exactly my wise-ass proclivities that Pessoa dislikes so that if he were alive, he would want nothing to do with me.

Nothing whatever. Nothing whatsoever! (Why is the second stronger than the first?)

Anyway, I am not the first to rouse Fernando from his big sleep. Saramago, their laureate in literature, has a novel called *The Year of the Death of Ricardo Reis*. No kidding. It's our Ricardo, Pessoa's Ricardo. The novel is Pessoan, needless to say, an odd meditation about perception and reality, ambition and fate, and the beauty and ugliness of existence. It is quite good and, had I read it before I began this, I'd have been too intimidated to compete.

But it's Reis, our guy. He comes back from Brazil and disembarks at Lisbon to visit Pessoa's grave, wander about the city, and say goodbye to it. And to life.

Pessoa's grave? It is also the grave of Ricardo Reis, whose being is inextricably bound up in Pessoa's. Pessoa is his father and himself. For him to survive Pessoa's death is a logical impossibility.

Impossibilities, however, are gifts, hints at how much more there is for us to understand. Or reminders that no matter how much or how deeply we understand, it will all disappear into what is, after all, an unimpressive *túmulo*.

It is raining and has been for a long time. Saramago reports repeatedly about the sounds of rain on roofs and on streets and about the heaviness of the air that is Lisbon's atmosphere. And beyond Lisbon, it becomes the atmosphere of existence.

Pessoa died the year I was born. This is suggestive, but I am not inclined to exploit the concinnity. It is too literary. (I am pleased to find that there are limits to my toleration of some of my fancies.)

Fictional characters may not ever die but they seldom reappear, continuing to act or speak or think after the death of their authors. Whether he knows it or not, Reis is particularly vigorous, having done this twice. His manner is not especially proud and he does not put on airs. He sits in his chair, mostly, and looks out of the window in the Hotel Bragança, as Bernardo used to do from that of his room on the Rua dos Douradores that so many of Pessoa's wraiths frequent.

As a group, these heteros are mostly sedentary, because to act would be for them to concede primacy to what you and I would call external reality, and this they disdain. There is a psychiatric condition in which the patient supposes that only he is real and everyone else is a mere figment. It stands to reason, then, that for a figment the people walking below his window must seem like real beings. This would not be altogether crazy.

Someone else's words in your mouth? It's an odd idea but actors do it all the time. And all of us, one way or another, are actors. Think of communal prayers, in which a number of people sit or stand together, reciting aloud what is in the prayer book in their hands. God has heard these words before, so the object cannot be to communicate with him. The movement is in the reverse direction and the purpose of saying the words aloud is to have them sink into the soul, the mind, or at least the tongue and teeth of the worshiper in a kind of osmosis. It must be of some benefit to some people, offering them tranquility, virtue, and peace.

Not for me. I am beyond such easy salvation. Above or beneath.

Before the written word, there were bards who went around from town to town reciting poetry they had memorized. From Homer, say. And as I consider this, I suspect that for the listeners, despite the fact that they knew better, the bard became Homer, at least in that moment and that place. This is even likelier if the guy was any good. It can happen on a stage or in front of a fire around which the audience is huddled, entranced. "The wrath of Achilles, Peleus' son! Sing, goddess…"

If the goddess is the one who singing, then we must understand that the words are hers as much as Homer's. He is only the amanuensis. As was Moses.

There were no amanuenses before there was writing.

Senhor Reis. May I ask you something.

"How am I to stop you, given our odd circumstances?"

You are a character created by Fernando Pessoa and you also appear in José Saramago's novel. And now this one, too. How is this possible?

"It is not a problem. Imagine that I am a character in Book A. Just that one book. But two people are reading it, or perhaps even more. I can be doing one thing on page 37 and quite another on page 133. So I can be in two different places at once. I am in London in one copy of a book, and at the same time in Bucharest in another copy. Now suppose that a reader likes the book enough to want to reread it. Not immediately, but a month or two later. I am again doing these things exactly as I did them before, saying the same things and thinking the same thoughts. Or thinking anything I like as long as I keep my thoughts to myself."

Are you joking?

"I can never be quite sure, but neither can you."

He bows his head slightly to indicate that the exchange is over.

There is just enough truth in the world to make lying amusing.

Let us step back for a moment to consider metempsychosis as it occurs in ordinary experience. (What is ordinary experience?) You are at a baseball game, let us say. (I have just said.) The players are in uniforms to show which team they belong to. On the backs are numbers, to show who they are. At away games, their names appear above the numbers. Without the names, we can differentiate among them only by consulting the program. Now let us suppose that in the locker room, there has been a mix-up, and two players are wearing the wrong shirts. A has B's number and B has A's. They have exchanged identities.

Or look around in the stands. People are wearing t-shirts that proclaim names (other than their own). There can't be that many Ralph Laurens in a random crowd. But despite the odds, there they are. As are a number of people named Harvard or Michigan. Or Bunker Hill Community College. (You'd have to be fairly stupid to wear such a shirt, but that is as it should be.) A number of people are Elizabeth Warrens. Few are Al Frankens anymore.

No, I am not being ridiculous. Beneath the letters and the fabric, beneath the skin even, there is an assertion of identity, an investment of the "real" self into the other, the fanciful, aspirational self. A small transposition, admittedly, but not insignificant. The ability was there in all of us when we were children and could for minutes or hours at a time become John Wayne or, at least briefly, Peter Lorre.

Reis returns to his hotel and is surprised to find someone in his room. So are we, because the visitor is Pessoa. Can this be? (Why not? It is fiction.)

Pessoa is real. Or was. Now that he is dead, he can come back (at least for a few months, he says). *Filho da puta*! He can be himself, of course, but Saramago does not specify the limits of his powers. I'd prefer it if he could be anyone he pleased—the Pope, for an afternoon, who could admit female priests, authorize divorces and abortions, and then disappear from the Vatican to return to the land of (different) shadows. (But that is another novel entirely!)

We imagine the land of shadows and have been doing so for millennia. Odysseus goes down to Hades to visit Tiresias and even if he is fictional most readers have taken it for granted that Hades is real. Nothing is hard to imagine although it is hard to imagine nothing. It is easier not to imagine nothing, but that is a feat of great spirituality that involves deliberately and willfully not thinking.

Saramago cheats. To summon Pessoa back from death, he allows for a nine-months transition, corresponding to the nine months we spend *in utero* because our goings out should be symmetrical with our comings in. Reasonable (but silly). And attractive. I wish I could believe it. I wish I could believe in Hades. And I wish for three more wishes.

Is "utero" a person who comes from Utah?

There is a chambermaid at the Bragança, Lydia. Her purpose? To bring a little sex into Saramago's book. It's a mistake, I think. As a novelist, he can do whatever he wants, but even so, if my understanding of Pessoa is accurate, he and his heteronyms are celibate, both by inclination and on principle. Considering their dim view of existence in this world, it would be hypocritical of Fernando or any of his ilk to bring more lives into it, condemned to suffer the same affronts and outrages that they have endured. Propagation and regeneration would contradict everything they believe. Reproduction would be a denial of their faith in nothing. Theirs is the god of erasure ("Let there be darkness!" or "Fiat tenebra!"). He is like the relentless waves of the sea that undo whatever men may have presumed to scratch in the smooth sand, disfiguring and then quickly obliterating the disfigurement.

Saramago, a novelist, was constrained by the assumptions of the genre. Pessoa was defiantly not a novelist. *The Book of Disquiet* is as un-novelistic as a book can be. Nothing happens. Time does not pass or bring us either development or resolution. Just one damned thing after another. As in life, which is not subject to any literary conventions and, perhaps for that reason, is never satisfactory. Or even persuasive. Saramago's novel remains insistently conditional. There is no reason why Reis does not return to Brazil. He thinks about doing so and could on the page beyond the one you happen to be reading. He could also die on any page, as he does, more or less, at the end. (His death is an excuse for the novel to stop. But the ending is defiantly arbitrary.) [As most deaths are.}

But who am I to criticize a Nobel laureate? A nobody. A *ninguém*. A presumptuous intruder who is like the tourist who has spent a week in a city and thinks he knows all there is to know about it. My defiant reply is that I am the author. The auteur. The *hauteur*? If I cannot create impressive monuments, I can deface them. E.g., we will rename the author, put him in drag and henceforward refer to him as Sarah Magoo. To destroy is also a creative act (Bakunin, I think) and easier to do. With her silly name, she is much less impressive. (I, too, am also less impressive for having thought up such a stupid paranomasia, but I don't mind. I rather enjoy it. And I have much less to lose than Sarah.)

The novelist's intention could not have been to put in a salacious sex scene. (Salacious = good for sales.) There is a Victorian reticence about what actually happens in the bed in room 201. Even the foreplay is foreshortened. The memorable gesture is that when Lydia turns down the bed, she does not do so with the coverlet on an angle on one side but in parallel with the headboard, as she does for two people in a *cama dupla*. That is her shy invitation. And all Reis has done up to that point is briefly to put his hand on her forearm. As in an adolescent's erotic fantasy, that does it.

Pessoa's distaste for actuality is what killed him. Cirrhosis, from excessive drinking to which he resorted too often for its temporary oblivion. Had Reis been anything like his creator, he'd have staggered home, opened the door of his room after some difficulty with the key, sprawled on the bed and, without even taking off his shoes, fallen asleep.

Perhaps as a gesture of love—or could it have been contempt? —Lydia leaves a glass of water and an antacid on his nightstand for the hangover headache she expects him to have in the morning.

As we might have expected, Sarah is annoyed with me. I can understand that. I have not only changed her gender but have clad her in a shapeless housedress and (why not?) put pink curlers in her hair that her kerchief does not quite hide. I have equipped her with a mop, although I doubt that we will see her using it. Mere mischief? No, not mere. One of Pessoa's apothegms is: "The wise man is satisfied by the spectacle of the world." Really? Then let's see some acceptance. Show us your Buddhist tranquility, senhora. You cannot grouse without betraying yourself, and the amusing part is that you are too intelligent not to realize this. (You cannot quail either. Or duck.)

Perhaps this is why she has those frown lines marking her brow, making an accurate topological map of her soul.

The best comics do their acts straight.

Pessoa says somewhere that people who want to be understood can never be understood. (He worked on that, I think.) He then untangles it for us, explaining that those who wish to be understood are too complex for anyone fully to comprehend, while those simple souls capable of being fathomed never worry about how their thoughts may be distorted in the minds of others.

Neat? But that's the trouble with it. It is a display of wit, and we know he is in that room, alone at that table, imagining a vertiginous obscurity at the brink of non-being. That's the real puzzle. Solitaries like him adore puzzles as a way to pass the time. Apparent contradictions are like those twisted metal constructions that you must manipulate in a certain way to separate their two pieces.

I have sometimes toyed with the idea of non-being, mulling it in my mind only to find that all my 206 bones protest, insisting that we are here and may as well get used to it. Unto dust we will return soon enough. (And Sarah Magoo will come with her mop to tidy it up. The mop turns out to be useful even without her having to deploy it. Indeed, I should apologize for so literary a turn. Set-ups and pay-offs are inherently deceitful. Life offers a myriad of set-ups but then, like a child with attention deficit disorder, forgets what he intended and stares stupidly out of the window.)

Poor Portugal! Cunard named one of its liners after her, calling it the *Lusitania*, which was the name the Romans used for their province there. And a U-boat sank it. Lives lost: 1,198! So the first association with the old name throughout the world is catastrophe. It is right, then, that Pessoa, Soares, and the rest of them travel the streets of Lisbon feeling uneasy. In this city the tang in the air is not merely that of the Tagus but the subtler and more pervasive perfume of failure and existential chagrin. Even stupid Lisboans bear the burden of this wisdom, whether they are aware of it or not. (Lisbotluns? Lisboniana? Lisboñeros? Lisbovi? Lisboni? The Portuguese nickname for them, for whatever reason, is *Alfacinhas*—which means little lettuces.)

At my request, Soares has read Sarah Magoo's novel. (If Pessoa can appear in it, there is no reason why Soares can't read it.) I asked him what he thought of it.

"Boring," he said, "as it should be. Pessoa's life was boring. So was Reis's. So was mine. It was brave, I think, to risk putting readers off that way. But that is just what Pessoa and the rest of us would naturally prefer.

"Don't you hate it when someone at a party tells you all about himself, where he went to school, what he does for a living, how many children he has? A more pleasant companion says very little. Or even nothing. Which demands nothing from you in exchange. In an ideal party, nobody would say anything to anyone. The only sounds would be the occasional rattle of ice cubes in people's drinks, or the popping of corks as the bartenders open new bottles of wine. Such parties do not exist, but it is pleasant to imagine one.

"All those like-minded solitudes together in one place, aware of each other but neither imposing nor conversing, because in the long run what is there to say? If there were a heaven and a hell, they both would be like that, cleverly identical. For refined souls, mentally and spiritually equipped for it, it would be perfection. For the rest, it would be torture."

Readers are an intrusion, a violation of privacy of the characters in a novel. One may assume, then, that while the author wants readers, the characters do not. They resent us. And insofar as possible, they keep their secrets from us. Did you know that Captain Ahab had a brother Phil, who was a ship's chandler back in New Bedford, and that the two of them have not spoken in years? Of course not. Was Charles Bovary ever unfaithful to Emma? He might have been but he never lets on—he may not be such a fool as we have been led to suppose.

A novelist can assert that something happened, but he cannot deny that something else also might have happened, even something more interesting than the events in his narrative. Ebenezer Scrooge had a standing appointment every other Friday with a French dominatrix in a discreet establishment only two blocks from his house. Why not?

Yet again, you are wondering where this is going. I am probably repeating myself, but I risk doing so to assure you once more that it is going nowhere. Developments are inherently dishonest, departures from what we have learned of reality during every waking minute. We ignore all that at our peril. To deny it is to abandon reason. And for what? A series of fairy stories in which we never believed even when we were children. A bag of magic beans!

We ought to be wiser as adults, but one of the emotions inculcated in us is fear. What will happen to us tomorrow? Or in five minutes? To allay our terrors, we transport ourselves to an imaginary world in which things—even small things—can sometimes seem to make sense. The long-suffering couple will at last marry and live happily ever after, or might if there were an ever after. All we have is a snippet of the Fates' yarn, which is by no means infinite. But to say that they marry and live for a while, more or less happy, is not satisfying. Willing suspension of disbelief? No, no. The only things we can willingly suspend are our pants. And bridges.

If that is not good enough for you, close this book, put on your scarf and gloves, and go out for a walk. It won't be any better out there, and you will come to realize that. But the exercise may do you some good. Or not.

And everything around you will be real, if you prefer to think so. And can stand it.

I woke up this morning and there was a dull pain in my lower back. I must have slept wrong. Or perhaps I sat wrong in a badly designed chair yesterday and the muscles down there took exception. It is not serious. I expect it will diminish and even disappear by tomorrow. But it set me to thinking how my awareness of myself actually is myself. And if that is true, I have, this morning, become a pain in the lower back. At least it is a large part of my identity. Without it I would be another Soares, a more comfortable one, luckier, but different. This is an awkwardness philosophers try to wriggle past with their distinctions between substance and accidence. None of that will make the pain go away or help me to endure it. (Tylenol is better.)

(Is the question even more subtle? If I think of the pain as my possession, it is difficult to resist that I have received it as a gift and that, therefore, I am the Chosen One of pain. That is ridiculous, and besides I would be obliged to learn Hebrew.)

The philosophers' awkwardness is my opportunity. I cannot be Soares unless I am conscious of also being Guedes, Reis, Campos, and the others, who are all parts of me as surely as my dorsal myalgia. A self is indivisible, but it can be multiplied. But not by zero.

When I was younger and had not yet heard of Italo Svevo; I saw a book of his in a shop window and misread the title. I misread it as *The Confessions of Zero*. It wasn't, but that is a book I should be eager to read. (Unless of course it had only blank pages.)

We can be blinded by purposiveness. Birds and beasts look around themselves all the time, in fear of predators and in search of prey. But do they see what else is around them? If I am going to some destination, I must pay at least part of my attention to where I am and in what direction I am moving. Pure looking is a luxury, neither so burdened nor focused. I am free to notice the intricate carving of a porch baluster or the way a beveled edge of a shop window at that fortuitous angle works as a prism and produces a rainbow on the wall beside it. I proceed along streets and through parks as if I were in a museum curated either by maniacs or geniuses.

My only distraction is the involuntary way in which I imagine, even if only for a few seconds, what it would be like to live in this or that ordinary house. They are different from where I live and it follows that I might have become a different person, putting down roots and acquiring a relationship to this or that place as trees must do, whether or not they are aware of it. Better not to be aware of it. (What good would awareness be?) Better just to be there that way, unable to imagine anything else.

Pessoa's heteronymic pals may have been the natural result of the tension he felt within him, a tension all writers feel to some extent. He speaks of Cesário Verde, who made sure that the doctor he was consulting understood that his patient was not just any Senhor Verde but *the poet*. Pessoa finds this amusing and sad. As far as the doctor was concerned, Verde's poetry was irrelevant. The doctor's interest was directed rather toward determining whether the pain was from his gall bladder or his heart. Which was more important to him than any poetry. [James Dickey is said to have done this, letting doctors know that he had been the Poet Laureate of the United States, as if that might get him more attention and better treatment.]

It is no great leap then to the notion that there were two Verdes, the poet and the patient. [And two Dickeys] And therefore two Pessoas. Or possibly twenty. That he gave them names is also understandable. Poets name things. They are like Adam wandering about in the Garden looking at the birds and beasts and plants and naming them. "You are a rutabaga. And you are a rose." (But in what language, I wonder.)

For those who are not poets to be doing this would be peculiar. Or presumptuous. Or possibly evidence that they, too, are poets after all, even though they have never put pen to paper. A tree can be an apple tree even if it has not yet produced apples. As Adam might have suspected.

But he and Eve were not so good at naming their children, were they? In Hebrew, Cain means "Yes."

Pessoa says somewhere that it is the essence of his life not to be a protagonist. (Not true, and Saramago did not believe him nor do I. So Pessoa was a Cassandra.)

Enthusiasm is inherently vulgar.

Sarah Magoo's novel is too political. Pessoa eschews politics. Eschews them and espits them out. The election results in Spain take up a fair amount of space in his book. I doubt that Pessoa would have noticed elections in Portugal. If he ever looked at any of the newspapers on the racks of cafés, he would at most have glanced at the obituaries, most of which are accounts of what the relatives of the deceased imagined his life to be. Or wanted it to have been.

The deceased himself has no idea about his life. It never occurs to him to think about it. Which suggests that he may be a wise man. Wiser at any rate than his survivors—who are inevitably referred to as "loved ones" even though that is not always the case. But ask yourself where we get our ideas of filial and paternal love. From novels, mostly. As if novelists knew anything or were at all concerned about correcting their readers' dangerous misconceptions. (Which would limit the book's sales to a tiny number.)

And fraternal love? A joke, surely, and a tasteless one at that.

Cain agrees, thinking of course in Hebrew.

Too political and too plotty. (Can I call him a plotty-mouth?) Reis is served with a writ and interrogated by the security police, which is much too dramatic for anything with Pessoa in it. We are all atwit (or at least somewhat atwit), eager to find out what happens. Will they summon him back? Torture him? Try to extract information he does not have or, worse, doesn't know he has?

Vulgar piffle. (The vulgar piffle is a seabird seen mostly along the Greenlandic coast.)

It keeps raining in Saramago's novel. As if Lisbon were the Seattle of Europe. And Reis has a mild case of the flu, but he recovers fairly promptly. Even this is rather excessive. Saramago was right to admire Pessoa but he didn't learn enough from him to have a proper disdain for events. Not good for a Nobel effing laureate. (But from Portugal! The committee likes to reward writers from minor countries. To do so makes them seem smart, and fair, and catholic [even if most Swedes are Lutherans]. Very nice, but they have to settle occasionally for some less than dazzling luminaries. When was the last time you curled up with a book by Eyvind Johnson or Johannes Vilhelm Jensen? Carl Spitteler? Władysław Reymont for pity's sake? 'Fess up now. Have you ever heard of any of them?)

To observe that the prizes (Nobel's and all the others') are awarded capriciously is not to make headlines, though. What is of interest here is Pessoa's aplomb. He didn't just ignore the awards and honors, he disdained them as distractions and corruptions. That kind of spiritual equipoise is as admirable as talent—and far more rare. Ideally, the two should come together, so that the two—talent and indifference—are always associated. (Like a plum and a pluot?) The talentless do not have to worry about prizes, or if they do, we are amused.

Pessoa would not have wanted the prize. The money would have been irrelevant to his life. And the inevitable attention that comes with the award would have distressed him. All that celebrity does is attract the wrong readers, people unlikely to be receptive to his mode of writing and therefore unfriendly to the books and, ultimately, to him. He would have happily forgone the ten million

Swedish Krona to keep those people away. At arm's length. Beyond the reach of a forty-foot pole. Farther. (Our Farther, which art in heaven...)

The ideal reader does not exist. Each writer must imagine him and then write with the aim of pleasing him. Is it enough to prompt a wan smile on Pessoa's face to think of a non-existent heteronym writing for a fictive reader? (Or to consider the possibility that some fictive readers might prefer non-fiction, not just for the wordplay but because there should be some minimal filament connecting the book to the real world?)

Too involuted? Perhaps but writers are often involutionaries (like Proust, like Faulkner, like Bernhard). They are too refined to parade through the streets carrying banners and signs. They avoid causes of all kinds even though most of the shoppers in bookstores like to have some excuse for reading, which they suspect may be a frivolous pastime.

There will always be enough injustice in the world to meet the needs of those writers whose work depends upon it.

SAVE THE BOTSWANA VULTURES.

No kidding. Philatelists will recognize the phrase. It appears on five Botswana postage stamps. It is a cause with which I'm sympathetic because there is no appropriate action I can take. Whatever I do would be like giving up haggis for Lent.

Cholent is Jewish haggis. But Jews don't have Lent. (Even so, I wouldn't much mind giving up cholent for a brief period.)

It is likely that our wish to leave something behind us is a mistake. We fear death and therefore try to imagine some part of ourselves that will survive, some faint trace. That, too, is an unexamined desire. It assumes that what remains of us will be creditable, fragments of our best selves. Why not make the fantasy a little more plausible and, if we are to posit the survival of some shard of our being, let it be an honest one, which is to say representative.

But that is a less attractive prospect, isn't it?

Indeed, the Pessoan position would be darker than that, his expectation being that the trace we leave behind would be something in the nature of a taint—because our lives sully the world.

Garden supply stores, some of them anyway, sell wolf urine, which is a way of keeping deer and rabbits from nibbling your parsnips. Poor Farmer McGregor never heard of such a thing. (Or Beatrix Potter didn't want to upset her young readers with such indelicate information.) But it is reasonable to suppose it would be effective. And more humane (and cheaper) than electric fences.

But the question arises as to how the deer and the rabbits know what wolf urine smells like. Most gardens are in places where there have been no wolves on the prowl for hundreds of years. How many rabbit generations would that be?

The smell is nonetheless still offensive. Or frightening to Flopseau, Trotseau, Queue-de-cotton, et Pierre. Which means that it is an enduring heritage.

Is that what we are hoping for?

That legacy of fear (and hatred) is not confined to animals. Humans react and behave in the same way. A friend of mine whose family came over from Sicily once told me that when he was a child, his parents would threaten that if he didn't behave they would let the Moors get him. There haven't been Moors in Sicily for several centuries, but they survive as bogeymen.

Are the ghosts of the Moors aware of this? And if so, are they pleased? Or can we imagine that, as ghosts, they have acquired enough wisdom to regret their depredations of the *undicesimo*? No, probably not. After all, they taught the Sicilians to make majolica ware. And marsala. Does this balance the accounts?

Of course not. There are no accounts.

Soares says something Pessoa was unwilling to say himself—that to begin a piece of prose is not brave in any way. More probably, it is stupid, because one knows what work he is undertaking and how pointless it is. Finishing the piece is also evidence of weakness rather than perseverance, because on each page there was an opportunity to abandon it, which would have been the right thing to do, but he didn't have the heart.

He then confesses that his frequent descriptions of landscape and cityscape, his characterization of the weather, his tendency to insert parenthetical comments and embellishments are to disguise the failure of his inventiveness. When people meet and think they should say something, they often mention the weather, good, bad, or uncertain. I do that, myself, out of cowardice.

The raindrops on my windowpane form rivulets that descend and meet, increase in size and speed, and then plunge to the muntin at the bottom of the glass. (Or is it mullion?) Do they take the tracks established by raindrops in last week's storm? Or do the drops of each downpour pioneer new routes? I can sit for minutes watching them and wondering at them and about them.

Utter foolishness! But then I often utter foolishness.

I am a spectator of my own life. This does not mean that I am not interested in how my expectations are thwarted and my hopes dashed. I have, on the contrary, a scientist's fascination with yet another demonstration of the validity of my theories.
To my bitterest disappointment, then, I add a small measure of satisfaction in the uncanny accuracy of my predictions.

The only surprises come from favorable outcomes. These are

rare, however, and random. Outliers that we ignore to keep the results accurate, or at least in line with expectations. I can dismiss them as anecdotal. I will not live long enough to increase the data base to anything approaching reliability, so I must make these tweaks and adjustments and lie a little for the sake of truth.

I have long ago accepted this paradox, but it must weigh heavily on the minds of more innocent and earnest observers. These minor irregularities are how astronomers discover new moons and new comets as technology allows us to peer ever more deeply into space. Where the outliers wheel and rotate. (Outliers and out-li-ars? Nah, too easy.)

Closer to home, on earth and in my room, these quirks sometimes manifest themselves, and I must be careful not to allow them to deceive me.

Happiness is a blasphemy. Think how much of the world and of your personal history you must deny in order to be happy, even for a moment. You can see, you can hear, you can think, but to be happy you have to ignore all these sights, sounds, and thoughts. Or worse, acknowledge but reject and defy them.

The idea of the countryside is much more attractive than the countryside itself. To avoid the reality of the rural, one must walk the busy streets of a city, where nothing intrudes on what he imagines. Conversely, one can best appreciate urban life in a large, gently sloping field in which crops stand ready for harvest. These are not willful paradoxes or perversities. One cannot help his feelings, which are sincere no matter how wrong-headed.

Thus, for Caeiro to be a shepherd in the countryside would

be of no interest to anyone. In the city, however, with his business cards and his shepherd's crook, he shows a certain flair so that he is worth at least a glance.

To what more can one aspire in this life?

NINE

You are not thinking *about* anything. Or to put it another way, you are not trying to solve some problem. There is no practical application for your cerebrations but rather they are free, spontaneous, and quite unexpected. You wake up in the morning and as the light of consciousness dawns in your mind, you find yourself wondering what the difference is between coddled eggs and shirred eggs. (Two eggs, any style? I'd like one coddled and one shirred, please.) Or more fancifully, what could Matthew have meant about the last being first and the first being last. We get the general idea, but how would that work?

I see a line of souls waiting to be judged, and the guy in the front goes to the back while the guy in the back goes to the front. Nobody else moves. Surely, that can't be right. (You go from 1, 2, 3, 4, 5, to 5, 2, 3, 4, 1. All those in the middle remain where they were? Do the first and the last just run around in an ellipse (the line is longer than it is wide), changing places, while the rest look on in puzzlement or, after they have figured out what is going on, resentment? Or contempt. It would make more sense to reverse the entire order, from 1, 2, 3, 4, 5 to 5, 4, 3, 2, 1. Or the first to go to the back of the line while everyone else moves up one place. But that messes up the neatness of the Biblical epigram. "The first shall be last and the last shall be penultimate" just doesn't have the snap. Even if we change the Latinate "penultimate" to the easier "next-to-last," it will still befuddle those whose gifts for math are minimal. [And no matter how you arrange it, #3, the one in the middle, stays put and has no idea what the others are doing, running so busily around.]

The first shall be last and those who are good at math shall be first? That can't be right, either. The first shall have shirred eggs and the last shall have coddled. If there are any eggs left.

These thoughts have the purity of uselessness. They are diverting and decorative. But grandly they are without any point. The value they have is that they come from nowhere and go nowhere. We have no idea how or why they arose in our minds. From our inner selves? Our truer selves? The selves we would be if we never had to balance a checkbook, let alone earn a living. The only other possibility is that they come from somewhere—or someone—else. All of Soares's thoughts (and many of mine) come from Pessoa, but where do his come from?

It is highly unlikely, but if we were interrogated on the matter which of us could definitively prove that he was not an invention of some Portuguese writer?

The lost shall be found and the found shall be lost. Was that what Matthew intended to say? The choreography would be less puzzling and the assertion is more rueful and more suggestive. That doesn't mean it is true but only that it ought to be.

There is a curious connection between the two Portuguese laureates. Saramago and Egas Moniz were both pioneers in nihilism. Annihilation is a rare ambition, requiring an exquisite sensibility for someone to devote himself to it. Pessoa, we might suggest, was Saramago's amusement, but his interest had been quite reasonably aroused. Or his need. For he, too, found himself lost in the middle of that *selva oscura* and in despair (the requisite attitude for the pursuit of nothingness) as he found Pessoa's faint track and began to follow it.

Egas Moniz, meanwhile, developed a medical procedure

akin to that of voodoo priests, boring holes in his patients' heads through which the evil spirits could escape. The wicked spirits were gone, but also much of the mental capacity and thus much of the person. Often, there was next to nothing left. He did not indulge himself with dancing or face painting and there were no chickens for him to whirl around his head, but still the patients' personhood had been obliterated. (That was collateral damage.)

The procedure has been mocked over the years as a cure worse than the disease, but the conditions it ameliorated were terrible. It was not even ironic but almost predictable that in 1939 a schizophrenic patient shot Egas Moniz repeatedly so that the psychosurgeon was thereafter confined to a wheelchair. (How did the schizo get hold of a gun? Not a shotgun, probably, because they are hard to conceal. A pistol, then, or a pocket revolver. We can imagine a solution to that minor problem. The schizophrenic did, which is what counts.)

Or one could say that Moniz had found a way to define non-being as a kind of health. At least the maniacal fits, rages, and deep depressions could be relieved and that could be considered as a kind of modest progress. Pessoa, Saramago's hero, would have supposed that existence was the disease, any amelioration of which was progress.

Most religions take it for granted that the creation of the universe was a good thing. There is no real evidence for that view. It could have been a cruel joke, because God was in a bad mood that day. Or there is no need to take it all so seriously. I can imagine that it could have been just a prank. He saw that it was good? Wink wink, nudge nudge. How can we be sure He wasn't suppressing a thunderous, universal guffaw astronomers mistake for the big bang?

The medico meant well, and there can be a persuasive case for what he did. You have to remember that insane asylums were horrible places back then, even the best of them. Egad, Egas, truly ghastly. And if there was a procedure, however risky, that would calm the patients so they were docile enough to be released and sent home, it is undeniable that the quality of their lives would have been much improved. Could it go wrong? Of course. But many operations have a significant risk. The doctor is obliged to explain these risks, and after that it is up to the patient or his family to decide. They are the ones playing the game; the doctor is only the dealer.

Even so, Egas Moniz's reputation is less than shining. There was a movement (there may still be) to try to get the Nobel committee to revoke his prize because of the damage he did to so many of his patients. (Nobel, remember, invented dynamite, which has sometimes done harm. And he also owned the Bofors Company, which makes cannons that cause a great deal of destruction if they are used properly.) What most people associate with the operation is disturbing: it is the outcome for the protagonist in Ken Kesey's *One Flew over the Cuckoo's Nest*. And it didn't help Rosemary Kennedy, JFK's sister (but here, too, we have to remember that she was mildly retarded before it was performed).

But by the time she was lobotomized the methodology had undergone significant changes. Dr. Moniz, as precisely as he could, drilled little holes in the head and then with a tiny knife severed the nerves that run from the frontal lobes to the rest of the brain. This was time consuming, and there was no evidence that the results were significantly better than, say, just going through the eye socket with an ice pick that one hammers in with a mallet and then randomly shmooshing up the prefrontal lobes. Strangely, that worked just as well. There was no theory, after all. And nobody knew what he was doing—neither Moniz nor his follower, the rather impromptu Dr. Walter Jackson Freeman II of The George Washington University Medical School. (The random shmoosh was also a lot quicker to do.)

[In 1950, Freeman performed the transorbital procedure in a motel room on an unwilling patient, whom the police were holding down. This tall tale is apparently true and invites comparison with the nearly fictional Dr. Benway in William Burroughs's *Naked Lunch*, in which that doctor in an operating room asks in angry eloquence, "Who cut my cocaine with Sani-Flush?"]

Very few lobotomies are performed these days—they are no longer fashionable but that is because there are now psychopharmacological ways to calm agitated patients. Or to perk up somnolent ones. There is also electroshock therapy. There are risks with these treatments, too, but less dramatic ones. Look at the side effects enumerated on one of their enclosures: "Angioedema of the face, extremities, lips, tongue, glottis, and larynx has been reported, which can be fatal if laryngeal stridor or angioedema of the face, tongue or glottis occurs causing airway obstruction."

Does that sound like fun? Especially the laryngeal stridor, which is altogether different from pharyngeal stertor. (But when you are gasping, trying to breathe, and making noises like those of a drunken frog, you care less than usually about these linguistic distinctions.)

We can, *en passant*, wonder about the tiny type in which these enclosure warnings are printed. Four-point pearl, or even smaller. Is it to avoid alarming the patients? Or is it to lull them into taking the medicines, because that is how the drug companies make money? Such questions are best left to medical ethicists, but we are not reassured. Ethicists are philosophy PhDs who could not get hired by a philosophy department (even for non-tenure-track positions) and wound up in hospitals where they get to tell doctors what to do and not to do. Or to suggest, one should say, for the doctors are always free to ignore them. (The doctors could pose these problems to lawyers, except that they hate lawyers, who make so much mischief with their pesky malpractice suits. The lawyers also have more authority because while there are many different philosophies there is only one code of laws about which to wrangle.)

It is always darkest before an execution: then it gets darker.

It could not have been in Egas Moniz's mind, but a poet's intentions have little to do with the finished work of art. This holds true in medicine as well. Figure that one of Moniz's patients was reduced to the mental level of a Brussels sprout. What then? An almost ideal Pessoan retreat into non-being, whether the surgeon understood this or not. And practically speaking, the life before the lobotomy could not have been tolerable. An unexamined life is said to be not worth living, but if it is both unexamined and wretched, both for the patient and family members (and the servants, too, I'd imagine), any escape from it would be both sensible and kind. A gift, really.

We must recognize that Moniz was a decent man, an idealist even. When he was the Dean of the Medical School of the University of Lisbon, he was arrested several times because he had tried to interfere with the police, who had been especially brutal in the suppression of student strikes. He was admired enough to have been appointed as Ambassador to Spain, and he served as Portugal's representative at the Versailles Peace Conference of 1918. A statue of Moniz stands in a courtyard somewhere in the Lisbon University School of Medicine. And the Egas Moniz's Siphon (the passage of the internal carotid artery through the interior of the temporal bone) is named for him.

He was, then, hardly a quack or back-alley desperado performing abortions and sewing up mobsters who have been shot. His reputation, nonetheless, is tarnished, even though the lobotomy could not possibly have been a result of any trivial nihilism on his part. The opprobrium may not have been deserved, but it clings to him and he should have the benefit of it. The mind? We almost certainly overestimate it. And, more important, the soul. Did that, too, fly out of Moniz's little holes? The Catholics think not, I believe. (The Catholics believe not, I think.) That is why they are generally good about idiots and crazy people. Their view is that the soul is a separate entity, probably less blemished in an idiot or a lunatic than it might be in the rest of us. If God loves them, who are we to argue?

At any rate, Pessoa, Soares, Saramago, and I can welcome Moniz into our study group. In error, perhaps, but as Freud maintained, there are no errors. Whatever is, is, however it came to be. Accidents and coincidences are simply labels we give to happenings we do not understand.

Good and evil? That's an easy call. Good and better cannot be so handily distinguished. And better and best? All we can do at that level is guess.

Let us return to the table in Soares's room on the Rua dos Douradores. (Have we ever left it?) Nothing that happens there is apparent, but there are thoughts, connections, constructions. For instance, the idea of leaving that room and that street seems impossible, but it would be as accurate to say that for Bernardo to get up and set out for the unknown, which he knows to be impossible, would be a journey to Impossibility. An Odyssey. A Lusiad. A Ramayana. Bernardo knows that he is not an epic hero, but he is at liberty to imagine himself venturing. Adventuring. Into another and probably grander realm. (For an instant, he feels the exhilaration Vasco da Gama must have experienced.)

Do I mean any of this, or am I just writing at random, hoping from time to time to persuade myself that I have stumbled onto something? How else do we write? How else do we live?

The trouble is that thoughts usually occur to us in words, and words are so misleading that they often corrupt the thoughts.

Again in the room on the Rua dos Douradores. But this time it is Pessoa sitting at the table. And he cannot imagine getting up and leaving. The best he can do is to imagine Bernardo imagining it. A wave of wordless sadness comes over him. He cannot decide whether it is on account of Bernardo or himself. Bernardo ought to have learned by now to give in to the hopelessness Pessoa has been cultivating and trying to teach him. Or call it acceptance. (Clarity of vision? In his dejection, he is unlikely to make so grand a claim.)

Sometimes it is all he can do to imagine getting up from the table and walking the five steps to the window from which he can look out at the defiantly banal cityscape. If that were the cause of his misery, he would have to admit to self-pity, which we are taught to avoid. (By whom? Our parents? Did they never feel sorry for themselves? Or were they setting a higher standard for us on the off chance that progress, even minimal progress, might be possible from one generation to the next. That supposition is depressing, and we feel bad for our parents, too.]

Nonsense. Just take it as it comes—whatever *it* is. We have, after all, no choice, even if we think we do. We are like characters in a novel who have begun to suspect that there may be an author and that he may have an outline he has been following.

Would this further burden Raskolnikov or would it free him? We have more important problems to consider.

All this while the pen in Pessoa's hand hangs motionless over the paper. He should be thinking about the next sentence, but he has been slightly distracted by the rhythm of his breathing and the barely perceptible pounding of the artery in his ear that, in moments of silence, records his heartbeat as from a distant jungle drum. (The heartbeat of darkness?) None of this means anything, and yet it means everything, for without these pianissimo noises there are no thoughts and there is no next sentence.

That disproportion, of which he is only intermittently aware, reminds him of the vanity of his undertaking, the delusion that is required to sit this way at a table, sometimes for minutes and sometimes, when the work is going well, for hours. (But think how many hours Dr. Johnson put in at his table writing the dictionary in which he sometimes must have found it difficult to believe. Hence "The Vanity of Human Wishes.")

Pessoa could be writing all this down but he chooses not to. And the perversely independent pen point pends.

The Tagus flows into the sea. But of course it is not that simple. There are stretches near the mouth of the river that are sometimes fresh water and sometimes salt, depending on the tides. There is, one might say, a dialogue between river and ocean, as there is between winter and summer or day and night. Any moment in these exchanges is temporary; what lasts is the alternation, which is ongoing but only discernible over time.

The senses, reporting one thing or another, are deceptive. Only the intellect and the imagination come anywhere near to the truth.

And their dialogue—that between the senses and the intellect—is less orderly than the cycles of nature and less reliable.

Which do we trust then? Both. And neither.

In order to create, I destroy myself. Or, more accurately, I externalize myself, creating my collaborators. So much have I done this that little remains of me. I am an empty shell, the stage on which various actors appear to perform in scenes they improvise. I can offer director's notes, but these are only suggestions they may or may not accept. This would be vexing if there were enough of me to be vexed.

Questions for contemplation:

What is the difference between squinches and pendentives?

Is jojoba oil better on your face than shea butter? Or cocoa butter?

What is black salsify and how is it different from plain salsify?

What are walking onions and how far can they travel in a year?

I could look up the answers, but all that would accomplish would be that I'd have a few more odd bits of useless information (useless bits of odd information). Left as they are, these questions and others like them are small windows into the world of indeterminacy, slight glimpses of what is infinitely more valuable than descriptions of rattlesnake beans or Burdekin plums. Or not even windows but, say, fissures, through which there are indistinct wisps, which, if I stare at them fixedly, begin to diminish like morning fog. And behind them, I can almost see the primordial blackness that is at the heart of things.

It would not be laziness, then, but hope that would prevent me from consulting architectural or horticultural texts for trustworthy information. How much better, how splendid to decide, simply as an act of will, what an answer might be and then find out, months or years later, that I was right! To discover that the world had conformed itself to my preferences, even in this minuscule matter and even if only at random. To imagine something, to conjure it out of thin air, and then to find it in space and time where others take it for granted and depend on it is to share in a tiny measure in what God supposed was His private amusement.

Were you aware that there are six varieties of lemons, if you include the yen ben lemon that is grown in New Zealand for export to Japan?

Would I make that up? (I wish I were that clever.)

"Thy will be done on earth as it is in heaven." The prayer's formulation is wrong, for "earth" and "heaven" should be reversed. If there are no gentle hills there, no tree-lined paths, blue seas dotted with islands and all the other pleasurable things, what good is heaven? For heaven to turn out to be nothing at all would be an eternity of absence—like what we have been studying here.

The conqueror, having achieved his aim, is no longer dissatisfied. Paradoxically, he accepts the world. Only victims, losers, and malcontents have any reason to strive for themselves and their fellow men. This gives them a sense of purpose that the conqueror can only remember (less and less vividly).

What then can he do? His best option would be to abdicate. The mere preservation of his achievement is no great undertaking. It is rather like housekeeping with the scrubbing and dusting that must be done again and again in an endless (and sordid) struggle against deterioration and disorder. He is weighed down by his victory as if by a load of jewels.

If I may venture a comment (and who is to object?), this is rather more high-flown than the meditations of Soares or Pessoa that, if not down-to-earth, do not usually swagger. Pessoa knows this because I know it. (Even Saramago must sometimes suspect it.) The passage is not inauthentic but uncharacteristic, which means that another character must be speaking. A recognition of this dissonance, I think, is how the assortment of heteronymics came to be. If it is not Guedes or Caiero, it must be Álvaro de Campos, who has been trying to decide whether or not to have another coffee. He does not actually want coffee but rather an excuse to sit for a while longer at this table under the shade of the green awning but with a clear view of the brightly sunlit *praça*. A glass of sparkling water perhaps? With a wedge of lime!

He may not be correct in his (unspoken) assumption that life should not be led according to principle or even reason, but according to taste. It is the unrefined life that is not worth living. This is not Pessoa's view or mine, but in the end, with all other strategies having demonstrably failed, we cannot assert confidently that his frivolity is wrong. (Truth, itself, may be frivolous. Why not?)

It is entertaining to imagine how clergymen would respond. Or philosophers. Aristotle was an intelligent fellow with many valuable insights, but where is his treatise on the servant problem—about which wars have been fought?

It is likely that when I expropriate the personality of some random

acquaintance to put it (him) to use as an element of one of my created comrades, I go further than I should and inadvertently learn
more about him than he understands about himself.

Coming into a room for the first time, we have a more vivid
impression than do its familiar occupants for whom it is fading
even as they stand there with their drinks in their hands. We see
more than they do, or more clearly. (Is that the same?)

A similar process sometimes produces surprising results—that
from the point of view of a heteronym I can see aspects of myself
of which I was previously unaware. What does Soares think of me?
He is too polite to say so, but there must be habits or locutions of
mine that he finds annoying. But he doesn't have to say anything.
I am him, after all, and can think his thoughts. Words are unnec-
essary and irrelevant. Tact, therefore, is useless. I know his mind
from the inside. And I can look through his eyes at my face in a
mirror.

What I see can be unsettling. And most of the time is depressing, as I would have expected.

Do I need a haircut?

The persistent problem is how to be insincere, sincerely. No, it is
not a contemptible and inane piece of wordplay. As silly as it may
seem, it is perfectly nane. It poses fundamental questions about
our attitudes toward other people and the entire external world.
The difficulty is to go about our business as if it mattered, as if
we believed in it. The continual temptation is to forget its mean-
inglessness and to take it seriously, although we know better. But
we cannot keep that in mind as we walk from the apartment to
the office. Our bodies move along in space and time and we are
seduced into supposing that these activities are what life is about.
What life is.

It demands constant vigilance to keep from slipping into the banalities of other men's absurd assumptions.

We are in a dessert, then, and have been trudging along for days on the burning sands, which we know are real. We do not have to be reminded. And yet there are mirages, oases, palm trees, tropical fruits, and the other paraphernalia of fantasy. It cannot possibly be. We are too intelligent or just too sane to take notice of the vivid landscape of that alternative reality, but only with great effort can we keep from running, or at least walking faster, toward that attractive delusion we know we shall never reach. And as we know, running—exertions of any kind—will only hasten our deaths.

Vultures circle overhead. We can see them. But we dismiss as insignificant their message, which is eloquent and clear. Perhaps they, too, are mirages?

These vultures are not endangered. The problem is that no one believes in them anymore. We have eyes but we see not.

Sea knots: the reef knot, the rolling hitch, the clove hitch, the sheet bend, the bowline, the figure-of-eight knot, and others, too, I'd imagine.

I'd apologize, but I am not responsible. I doubt if it was Pessoa or one of his swarm of alter egos. Who is left then? My guess would be that it's Saramago, inserting himself and trying to embarrass me because, as he sees it, I have been making light of him. Slighting and inciting him. He is dead, of course, but so is Pessoa. (Those other gentlemen never even condescended to live.) There is no way to prove it is not Saramago. Or that there are no green polar bears.

José despised such bad jokes when he was alive. Dead, his sense of humor has diminished even further. (But it is not entirely gone. He was able to segue from *see not* to *sea knot* rapidly enough. Even if it was mean-spirited, it was nevertheless spirited. So who knows what he's capable of?)

One of the quirkier aspects of Saramago's novel is that from time to time Dr. Reis and Senhor Pessoa meet to discuss life and art. I feel entitled, then, to converse with any or all of them. Saramago has Pessoa talking about existence after death. (There has to be some kind of shadowy existence to allow him to revive, appear, go for walks, and chat with Reis, his creation and nonce interlocutor.)

I am not surprised that Saramago is annoyed, but what can he do to me? In American law, you cannot libel the dead. (English law, I think, considers a man's reputation to be his property and therefore part of his estate, so his heirs can sue for libel, but this does not happen often.)

He is uncomfortable with sea knot. I appeal, however, to a sentence in *The Year of the Death of Ricardo Reis*, "If we do not say all words, however absurd, we will never say the essential words." Yes. Profoundly trivial and trivially profound.

Truth, if there is any, must lie on the cusp. (And if not, there is always the cuspidor.)

When he wrote the novel, Saramago was alive. (Obviously.) But Pessoa was dead. It was therefore necessary for Saramago to imagine deadness, which is an impossibility. He makes Pessoa's wraith gnomic and epigrammatic, although there is no reason to suppose that the dead are all doing impressions of Oscar Wilde. (The pinnacle of heaven cannot possibly be *Lady Windermere's Fan*.) [Or can it? Do angels ever quip?]

I am not being fair, am I? What Saramago has to do for perfectly sensible reasons is to suggest somehow a different tessitura, a slightly mannered conversational style that is neither normal nor altogether weird. The dead should not sound like you and me. Thus, the epigrams that were the best Pepe could do. (Yes, Pepe is the diminutive for José. I don't know why [he swallowed a fly/ Perhaps he'll die].

So I ask him the question only gauche people dared put to him when he was alive. (It is not clear to me that he is now less likely to be offended, although that is what I risk.) What was it like, getting the Nobel Prize?

"It was fine. Some money. Some celebrity. A modest increase in the sales of my books. But it wasn't without its disadvantages. People made too much of it and, of course, got it wrong. The academy recognized me as worthy, but they have made many mistakes. Pessoa never got the award, for example. And his work was better than mine. I kept that in mind so as to maintain a little skepticism. I still do. I didn't have the contempt for prizes Pessoa would have had but I understood that they are invitations to think too much of oneself. I was not any different after the prize than I had been before."

That sounds a little too good to be true, if you don't mind my saying so.

"It's true enough. But there is some truth in it, which is more than we get most of the time. And if I did mind your saying so, what could I do? You're doing the typing so it's your party. But if I may ask a favor, I'd prefer not to be called Pepe. I never liked it. Pepe sounds like a bartender."

That's the least I can do.

"No, the least you can do would be to go away and leave me alone."

You didn't object to Sarah Magoo?

"No. It was such a lame joke that it didn't bother me at all. You are the one who looked bad."

Maybe. Or that could be a part of my plan. If I let myself look bad now and then, some readers may think I am being straightforward and sincere. And therefore believable.

"Are you saying that good manners are always insincere?"

Yes, absolutely. And the more insincere they are, the more they are mannerly. Thank you for mentioning. It is rather Pessoan, is it not?

He does not answer. Content to leave it there? Or just bored? I can think whatever I like. As you can, too.

"A poet does not need his muses to speak but only that they exist."
–S. Magoo

Ah, but how would he know if they never speak? It works the other way, too. It works better. A poet does not need his muses to exist but only that they speak. Ridiculous? Sure, but closer to the truth than the other way. Writers are mostly intelligent people but we seem not to know much about what we are doing. It's embarrassing, really. Perhaps this is why Pessoa invented all of his alterities. People who do not exist seldom have reason to be embarrassed.

Think about it. You do something unspeakable. Spill the wine. Pass wind in an elevator. Whatever. And you want not to be there. You want to be one of those fortunate non-existent beings who can never be blamed for the gauche things they do and say. Let him who is without sin cast the first stone? (It's a joke, I think, because anyone without sin would be unwilling to cast a stone, no?) But those non-being beings are without sin and the worst they can do is imagine flinging stones. But wait, it is "casting stones," isn't it? A sculptor could make a cast of a stone and from that produce a bronze object that would and wouldn't be a stone.

Tiresome? You can, if you choose, close the book. You could have done so long ago. And you can come back to it or not. You are not condemned to it, as I seem to be. Do you not suppose that I might prefer to be writing from insights that are both profound and useful? And so beautifully expressed, too. But no, I am condemned to this persiflage because I am that kind of person. And we do not get to choose ourselves. Rather we discover our selves, one disappointment after another and we learn as well as we can to settle. The alternative is self-hatred. Depression. Catatonia. (Homage to Catatonia!)

So, we'll make a deal. I'll forgive you and you'll forgive me. (We won't, really, but we can pretend, which is [marginally] better than nothing.) (About which, much ado.)

TEN

Yimach shemo v'zikhro!

It is a Hebrew curse: *may his name and his memory be oblit-erated.* It is appropriate for Amalek, Haman, and Hitler, the worst curse a Jew can frame. Pessoa, however, said that that was what he wanted...for himself: "If only...I could be absolutized into Dark-ness, so that not so much as a shadow of me would remain that could taint, with my memory, whatever lived on."

I cannot think of an example of greater self-loathing. This has to be the zenith or the nadir or the *nec plus ultra*, unless it is merely the logical extension of Pessoa's mood, all the more frightening for being formulated into words. Self-loathing and a loathing of the world. A distaste for existence, or an allergy to it, such that he wants no trace of its corruption to touch him or his shadow or memory. (Memories are our shadows in time, are they not?) [Are they? In Straus's *Die frau ohne schaten*, shadows are progeny, so that the woman without a shadow is one who has no children.]

Either way, what Saramago did and what I am doing defies Pessoa's clear prohibition and is exactly the opposite of his wishes. (Or those of his dummy Soares.) I can't speak for Saramago, but I can say confidently and categorically that I had no intention to do him harm. My only excuse—a flimsy one, I admit—is that he was an ironist (in the great laundry of the world) and therefore I could at least hope that he didn't mean it. Who would want his name obliterated and his memory's shadow to be erased?

You see how words always leave a little wiggle room. For this reason, the Zen masters do not rely on language. They hit. Very clear and unambiguous, the bite of the switch on vulnerable flesh delivers its message to the novice who has had the nerve and the bad judgment to ask a question.

There are, of course, books about Zen Buddhism. But they are in words and thus misleading. What readers need is a visit from an elderly, thin, bespectacled man in saffron robes who strikes with his stick whoever answers the door. And he comes back every week thereafter. (What is the sound of one hand hitting?) Eventually the door no longer opens for him, which is the beginning of common sense, if not of wisdom.

But say that the guy, A, sells his house to B, which could certainly happen. But the monk persists. He shows up one Thursday afternoon, rings the doorbell, and delivers a smart, open-handed slap to the new owner. This is unfair, because B has not asked a question. B is totally puzzled. As the monk makes his way back to the street, B calls out and asks, "Are you crazy?" (Possibly, but there is madness in the world and we must learn to accept it.) The following week, the unknowing and unwilling acolyte B asks, "What is going on? What are you doing?" The monk feels no obligation to respond because the man (now the pupil) may eventually discover what is going on, or at least learn to accept it so that the questions will stop.

Rain or shine, hot weather or cold, Junichiro appears on Thursdays. He goes to his barber on Thursdays to have his head shaved, and the house is conveniently around the corner. Realizing that the only way to meet absurdity is with another absurdity, B invites the monk in for tea. (They drink tea, don't they?) Junichiro does not speak but he smiles for an instant in recognition of progress before he turns away.

And then? And then? And then Soares yawns, puts the cap on his pen, neatens the pile of manuscript pages, and switches off the light.

Should I smile now in recognition of progress?

Absurd? I'll tell you what's absurd. The nausea I experience when I leave the apartment to go for a walk in the city. It doesn't make any difference which parts of the city I go to—the shopping districts, the residential areas, the parks, the riverbank. What I do there is eavesdrop. I am not interested in whole conversations or even whole sentences. Fragments are more than sufficient. And they are infinitely depressing and boring. The debased coinage of language is passed around from one person to the next, and neither of them seems to realize that the coins are worthless. Trite, predictable, un-grammatical—the errors in grammar are the least uninteresting of the things they say because a few of these are unprecedented. But most of the time, what I overhear is used thoughts garbed in used words. I set out in a foul mood that only gets worse.

The feeling, as I have said, is one of nausea. And the only cure for nausea is vomiting. One lies down, nibbles a salted cracker, tries everything to avoid the mess and stink of regurgitation, but the body has its own views—that the only way to get better is to get worse. The ordeal must not only be endured but must be invited. One goes to the bathroom, bends over the toilet bowl and disgorg-es the nastiness. Only then, relieved but exhausted, can he rinse his mouth out with water and lie down again, this time in a state of tranquil insensibility.

You know what I am talking about. If you have read this far, you, too, have felt the outrage and disgust I am describing. And the horror that you and these creatures are of the same species. That's what's absurd. Silliness is a refuge from these not-quite-human beings, if only because they do not have the inclination to follow you there. They are offended. They dismiss you and even condescend. There are other ways to hide, of course. In alcohol or drugs, for example, or in suicide. But the aim is the same—to avoid the unbearable assaults that lurk around every corner, float from one restaurant table to another, swirl from park benches, or invade like a miasma in the air above the streets and public buildings.

You didn't have to believe in him or take him seriously, but the idea of a Japanese monk showing up every week to hit someone chosen at random was appealing, wasn't it? Or its defiant foolishness was attractive. (Is there a difference?)

We are driven to such strenuous extremities by our despair and the intolerability of our situation and we never quite come to accept the inevitability of this pained reaction whenever we venture outside.

So, for the time being, back to the room, the table, the pen and paper.

And who was that? It is hard to tell. These words could have come from Pessoa, from one of his many heteronyms known or unknown, from Saramago, or even from me. But it doesn't matter. No one will want to take credit for such words. And no one can copyright the truth.

These are the least political people I can imagine. But that observation about the snippets of conversations one overhears everywhere and always has political implications that are difficult to deny. Granted that democracy is a good (Aristotle didn't think so, nor did Plato) or anyway a safe kind of government, the egalitarian principal should be confined to its proper sphere—voting, the courts, the business of citizenship. But people blur it to a dangerous generality that Huey Long invoked when he said, "Every man a king." How was it that nobody noticed the inherent self-contradiction of the slogan even as an aspiration? If every man is a king, nobody is a king. Or if we are all kings, we are engaged in a war of each against all—as kings mostly have been. There can be no laws, for each king is above the law, a law unto himself, an autocrat (albeit only of his own life).

One of the charms of the Pessoan view is that he makes each of us a king in exile and incognito, a king passing as an ordinary subject in order not to be arrested or possibly killed. His kingdom is hidden, internal, and theoretical. Confining but tolerable.

None of the heteronyms thinks in these terms, so what we are driven to suppose is that this is a new one. French perhaps, and a Bourbonist. (Are there any of these left? Probably in Kentucky.)

Should we name him then? But no, I think I have already conjured a creature into a shadowy half-life. Ferruccio, wasn't it? Silva the Minister of Culture of the current government. (What do ministers of culture do? The French have one, I know. And Melina Mercouri was the Minister of Culture of Greece. We don't have one in the States, but that may be because we don't have a culture. Only entertainment.)

You don't get a vote, anyway. Democracy is acceptable in politics but has no place in art. Or in this book, anyway, where *le monde c'est moi.*

Portugal used to have kings. My favorite? Pedro the Cruel. (No kidding. Look him up.) He was worse than "Ivan the Terrible" because he was pettier.

Saramago sets Dr. Reis on a journey to Fátima, for no particular reason. It is a whim either of Reis's or Saramago's. He/they get there and among the crowds of desperate/faithful, there are, of course, beggars. And in a particularly intriguing passage, Reis tries to distinguish between the fake beggars and the real ones.

Men and women of both groups are begging, so the distinction is merely one of theory or, say, of motive. The "real" beggars are the ones in terrible need. Without contributions from passers-by, they might very well starve. Despair is the hallmark of their authenticity. The others? The ones who are only posing as beggars, might have started out as real but they realized at some point that this could be a living as well as a life and they continued, jingling coins in the same cup and droning, "God bless you, God bless you." (At Fátima most of the pilgrims probably believe in God.) They had now become professional beggars. There is no way to tell them from the amateurs except by somehow intuiting their motives.

(Have you ever paused during a chase on horseback in a Western to think how John Wayne is acting while the horse he rides is not? The horse doesn't know this and neither, perhaps, does Wayne, but you do—and this separates you not only from the movie but more likely than not from the other members of the audience. There could be one or two men in the posse who have thought of this disjunction, during the long, boring moments of the setting up of the lights but they are only extras and have no lines of dialogue. It wouldn't matter anyway, because however large the posse it will be Wayne who catches up with the villains and all alone shoots it out with them on the rocky hillside.)

I lie awake sometimes wondering about the announcement on

some commercials that the people we are seeing are "real people, not actors." Are actors not real people? Or, more troubling, if they go out and find amateurs to do the commercials, do they not become actors the moment they assume their positions next to the shiny car and say their lines? And if that is true, then the logical conclusion is that there are no real people. Okay, even that is bearable. I am troubled nevertheless that these questions do not trouble everyone else.

No wonder Pessoa drank himself to death

About the beggars, Reis is asking the wrong question. Both groups are real. All we can say is that some are authentic while others are just acting. Probably there are those in the middle who are sometimes professional and sometimes amateur. Think of the gradations of whores, some of whom are only semi-pro and pretend, to themselves at least, still to be amateurs. They do not take money for sex, or at least they disguise the transaction, asking for ten thousand escudos (about $50.00 USD) to tip the lavatory attendant in the nightclub. The gentleman companion understands perfectly well what she is doing and gives the money. (A few may even tip the woman in the lavatory but much, much less.)

(*Mens rea* makes for messy jurisprudence.)

Reis comes to no conclusion about the beggars, but how could he? If he has any intention himself, it is in Saramago's head, as it was once in Pessoa's, and now is in mine. Or, for all I know, yours. With such paradoxes and conundrums, it is impossible for any of us to move even from the desk to the window. (It isn't "conundra," is it?)

Along with Zeno, we are paralyzed. But only if we think.

So? Don't think.

Possibly because he has been contemplating the degrees of the beggars' credentials, Saramago turns his attention a few pages later on to words, which are also sometimes true and sometimes not. The words in a lie will be just the same if it were a truth, and we have no sure way to tell the difference. We must forever be on guard.

A few words always lie. "Flammable" is such a word, invented to warn the sub-literate that the stuff in the truck can catch fire. They are confused by "inflammable" which means able to be inflamed but which some take as a negative of "flammable." (With confidence, then, they light up a cigarette and blow up not only themselves and the truck but the building next to it.) There are also the words of Dada-ists. Magritte's "This is not a pipe" comes to mind. But these are not lies so much as jokes. Their falsity is how they delight.

Then there is Alfred Korzybski's "The word is not the thing," which is true unless the word is the thing. This one, for instance.

(Don't you just hate it when one of those smart-ass assertions turns out to be stupid, which is only worse for the authority it claims by its brevity? Take "War is not the answer." High-minded, no doubt, and right thinking. Who could argue? Me! What if the question is "What do you call it when the armies of two countries engage each other in battles"? What the slogan on automobile bumpers ought to say is "War is rarely the answer," but while that is closer to the truth, it is less neat. Are truth and neatness natural enemies?)

You could think about using one of those spray-paint cans to obliterate the "not" so that the dove-ish bumper sticker is turned into an emphatically hawkish one. This is what Senhor Silva recommends.

His father, of course, was Portuguese, his mother Italian. She claimed to have had a beloved Uncle Ferruccio, but she might have been telling a small fib to give more credence to her passing whim. The only Ferruccio she ever knew was a little boy at the next desk back at school.

It is, in any case, a martial name. And it to some extent it may have shaped her child's character. It could also have been a coincidence that he was given to fights and quarrels in childhood and grew up to be contentious and impatient. He became a poet only to counter-balance the pantywaist simperings that were in vogue among the Portuguese versifiers and poetasters of his day. Critics (some of them other Pessoan creations) called him a "brutalist," and he blithely adopted the name and claimed to be a member of the brutalist group. (If there were others in the group, they were no less imaginary than he.)

Or you could set fire to their cars, he suggests. You don't do this yourself. It is safer to hire some punk kid. You won't have to pay a great deal. These ruffians do this kind of thing just for the fun of it. (If they get caught, the penalties for juvenile offenders are much less severe.)

All these ideas you fellows have are too complicated. To understand anything, you have to simplify, Silva says. Never mind about truth and lies, stop worrying about real and fake. Admit what is before you as if it were written on a huge billboard. What bothered Fernando Pessoa was deeper than those things. He was a disappointed rationalist. Nothing makes sense. There is no order. There are no causes and effects. We pretend otherwise, but we know we are pretending. He couldn't stand it. He rejected everything around him as stupid and inconsequential, which it is. But he was heartbroken about it, and furious. He was living the life of a survivor in a conquered city in which the human situation is made painfully clear. In the rubble and ashes of great buildings, men steal from one another and women sell themselves for cigarettes.

Some such scene was the mural in his mind, and it made the streets he traveled in Lisbon into a cruel parody. The bricks and stones were merely posing. The flowers were sarcastic. People were pretending that the world was at peace. Or at least that Portugal was. It is for that reason—or one just as bleak but in different words—that he worked on his book, a masterwork of disorder, determinedly incoherent.

If the sentences seem to flow in a discernible direction, the paragraphs do not. Why should they? For them to do so would be to assume—and proclaim—a rationale everyone knows to be an invidious dream. Bad enough that we are so deluded as to believe in it. Worse, we teach it to our children, blinding them to the nature of the lives they lead and the world they inhabit. These misconceptions are like a genetic disease we pass on from one generation to the next.

That is surely what tormented Pessoa and drove him to the edge of sanity where at least the scenery is distracting.

It is not utterly implausible, but I ask Silva how it could be that none of his heteronymic colleagues ever thought of that. (Or if they had entertained the thought, even briefly, had never mentioned it.)

"They—and Saramago and you—were all such good souls or, in other words, naïve. You were all looking for a civilized world and trying to prepare yourselves for it. You lacked the objectivity that is required to let you see what you are staring at. People can imagine goodness well enough. To imagine evil takes dedication and a hardiness of spirit. Evidently, none of you had it. Except perhaps Campos, the dandy who paid no attention to good or evil or anything that he could not discern through his monocle."

Or he guessed but he never mentioned it. The last thing in the world he wanted was to be useful. As far as he was concerned, usefulness and helpfulness were insufferably trite.

"That's where refinement gets you in the end."

That is perhaps a lapse in your thuggishness.

"I do my best to avoid wit. Or you do, when you are speaking for me. You should try plain speech once in a while. Say what you mean. Too often, you say whatever comes into your head and then consider whether you might have stumbled upon something interesting. Or even true." Silva displays a rictus of triumph that is as far away from a smile as it can be.

Literature, painting, sculpture, music… What good are they? They do not improve our lives. They don't even embellish them much. But we have the feeling that they are more than entertainments and somehow good for us. It isn't that they are soothing, for some paintings and some novels and poems are quite disturbing even while they are at the same time satisfying.

A possible solution to this problem is surprisingly simple: the arts take us elsewhere. In our dismal plight, otherness, however brief and illusory, is irresistibly attractive. The songs the sirens sang? We assume they must have been unbearably beautiful, but it is also possible that they appealed so intensely to Odysseus because his life was so full of pain. (As whose is not?)

The Baron of Teive comes back from the dead. If Pessoa and Reis can come back in Saramago's novel, Teive, too, can be a revenant. He was a latecomer to Pessoa's group and he committed suicide, which Pessoa described as the only logical outcome of his (Pessoa's? the Baron's?) gloomy view of the world. But then, wink, wink, the Baron continued to write. Or at least to publish. (Was there an imaginary Louis Vuitton steamer trunk somewhere full of manuscripts? Like Hemingway's?)

Just as with Soares, the Baron was a distorted self-portrait of Pessoa, and he is therefore as authoritative a spokesman as Pessoa could expect. He agrees with Silva about their creator's disappointment with the world. But he takes the idea further, suggesting that Pessoa felt betrayed by reality. Which means, the Baron explains, that he was, *au fond*, a disillusioned idealist, which is a dangerous thing to be. All the hypocrisies and deceits we learn to accept (what choice is there?), Pessoa took as personal affronts. They caused in him a sharper pain than most of us experience as we let go of our childhood certainties and mature into our compromised and compromising selves.

Plausible, but we must remember that the Baron might be toying with us, just as Pessoa might have been doing. On the other hand, whatever their intentions, they might have been telling the truth, which would appeal to their extremely dry sense of humor.

Saramago's novel is not funny enough. To be an accurate representation of Pessoa or one of his heteronyms, there should be … Absurdities if not actual jokes. The funniest passage in *The Year of the Death of Ricardo Reis* is a description of an air raid drill, in which biplanes fly above Lisbon dropping smoke bombs over a panicky crowd, while an oblivious street-sweeper works his way along the street that an indifferent mailman crosses and recrosses as he continues on his route. The dissonance of their appearances is persuasively Pessoan, although the rest of the book is far too much concerned with plot and action, even if of a limited sort.

Reis does not seem comfortable in his resurrection. He goes through the motions (he has no choice) and he broods some (not enough) but the whimsy is missing. Whimsy was not Magoo's long suit.

> *You sewed the buttons strong,*
> *But Sam, you made the pants too long.*

Pessoa has interesting things to say about tedium, which is not at all interesting in itself. He observes that when one experiences tedium, he thinks without thinking and feels without feeling. Beyond spiritual weariness, there is a mindless disgust with everything. One is a captive in his own castle and can gaze out at the landscape, knowing that he can never set foot in those meadows or walk in those woods.

To suffer without suffering and want without desire is to be the shadow of a self. It is to be hanging in a limbo that is closer to hell than to heaven.

Whoever first thought up the idea of zombies must have experienced tedium. Must have been a connoisseur of it. And the popularity of zombies in books and movies is evidence that audiences share this experience and know it at least well enough to recognize it when they see it. Some of them even identify with the zombies as they gather at the cemetery gate, preparing to attack the city, the residents of which are so insufferably smug and boring.

The condition passes as mysteriously as it appeared. The self returns to resume its position on the bridge. Was it on break? Did it have to go to the lavatory? (Is there a head in the head?) What is going on?

This is a question most of us manage not to face most of the time, even though it pends and pends and pends, as constant as breathing.

Sane people are all alike. Crazy people are crazy, each in his own way. It's a better first sentence than Tolstoy's, but I am not going to continue and write a whole novel because of it. (About a delusional girl who thinks she is Anna Karenina?)

We are all more or less near-sighted or astigmatic. Only in our dreams do we see things in undistorted clarity. More to the point, people and objects are sharper and brighter according to how important they are to us.

The eyes deliver imperfectly their information to the brain when we are awake, but in our dreams the brain creates its own images, which we perceive at first hand. Memory and imagination collaborate to present to our consciousness glimpses of the world we actually live in, which is more attractive or frightening than the houses we inhabit and the streets we walk every day.

Such vividness all the time would be exhausting. Or call it a liveliness that would probably kill us.

One way to endure the bumps and bruises of life is to consider that everything that happens to us is an accident. Or that we are in a novel that someone else—not necessarily talented—has written. In no case are we responsible. We are not heavily invested in the narrative, which seems incoherent anyway. Take that as our underlying attitude and make it habitual. Thus, I think, we can achieve the indifference we need. We may not be happy but we should be able to avoid much of the misery with which each day assaults us with its deceitful sunrises, all rosy and peach.

We can look and even admire but we must not let ourselves be taken in.

I must learn to accept banality. There is so much of it everywhere. I don't have to approve of it. But I must at least acknowledge its omnipresence and try to contrive some way of accommodating myself to its tiresome iterations. Some day I may have learned not to be dismayed by the commonplace and I will be more comfortable (but less admirable).

I ought to say something about Saramago's title. It isn't *The Death of Ricardo Reis* but *The Year of the Death of Ricardo Reis*, which is slightly—drastically?—different. He makes references now and then to what is going on in 1936, the year he is writing about. Think of it: Italy and Ethiopia, the Germans, the Soviets, the appearance of ominous cracks in the foundations of European politics. From our vantage point, we can see what is coming. The disquiet that Pessoa, Reis, and the others are experiencing is not one for which any amount of alcohol can be an anodyne. It is nothing that even the best psychotherapist can relieve because it is not only inside Pessoa's head but also out there in the world. [It is not Freudulent.] The historical moment may or may not be the cause of Pessoa's nausea and we are left to decide to what degree his disgust was auspicatious.

All that in one word? Quite possibly. And if so, we must admire the economy of the author's means for achieving so great an effect. For all I know, though, this is just my reading of his book and its intentions. I could be more aware of these subtleties than Saramago was. (Not likely, but neither is it altogether out of the question.) Most of us do things, say things, or write things that we do not fully understand (or do not understand at all). The necessary consequence is that our feelings of uncertainty about the course of our lives ought to be more acute, more paralyzing so that we recognize in ourselves Pessoa's bitterness. If we are not so crippled by these feelings, it is only because the bandwidth of our attention is so narrow that we miss the obvious signals from the world outside our windows.

It is our fault. Pessoa was braver and more honest than we are. Which makes him a hero—the very last thing he wanted to be.

These imaginary writers must have been amusing to Pessoa, at least at first. But he seems to have lost interest in each of them after a while. Some persist for years while others fade away relatively quickly. My guess is that when their novelty wore off, they began to be boring. Pessoa would not have objected to that necessarily. He believed in boredom, both for itself and for how it can bring into focus tiny phenomena on which the hungry mind and eye happen to alight for a moment.

He walked a block and a half every morning to his job at the bank and every evening took the same short route in reverse. With a regimen like that, the street quickly became boring and he paid less attention to it. But then, in his ennui, he began to take notice of minuscule changes. Someone had left the lid off a trash bin in a narrow alley. So? At first he merely glanced at it. Then a few days later looking again, he saw the scurry of grey that meant that the rats had noticed it also. And then someone else must have seen a rat, too, because the next day the bin was emptied and the lid was put back on more securely.

In itself, the story of the trash bin is trifling, but Pessoa might have liked it for that very reason, because most of the things that happen in the world are on this scale. Activity is constant but unless you are in a receptive frame of mind, you are likely to miss it. Primitive men and women deep in the jungle are trained by their elders to see at this micro-level because their lives depend upon their ability to observe. Living in cities, we lose the capacity for alertness and, if our lives are no longer at risk, neither are they of any interest anymore.

Anxiety, depression, and a whole catalogue of neuroses are like childhood diseases. The chances are that we will outgrow them, if we live long enough. And if not? Then we adapt to them. Think of them as eczema of the soul.

And who said that? Well, I did, but it does not sound like me. I am beginning to think and to speak in ways that I have acquired—unconsciously, but that makes no difference—from Soares or Guedes or Reis. Which is to say from Pessoa himself. I must infer from this that Saramago's conceit of a resurrected Pessoa who comes to visit Reis and converse with him is not meaningless. Saramago must have felt it happening to him and therefore decided that it could also happen to his protagonist.

This mimetic capacity is a fundamental part of one's character. Children learn how to speak this way. Animals have the same ability: monkey see, monkey do. We parrot speech patterns and ape behaviors we find interesting. We try on gestures the way we try on clothes, to see how they feel and to judge how we look in them.

You could say (I am saying) that this is Saramago's basic concern in his Reis novel, one of them anyway.

As Álvaro de Campos might say (is saying), "I must think

about this." He orders an Armagnac to keep him company while he broods.

"All this is very high-flown, isn't it?" Ferruccio says. Shaking his head in a slow, definite "No," he sighs as if in weariness. "You seem to think that you need refractions and reflections in order to look at something. Most of the time, all that is necessary is that you stare at it. You seem incapable of simplicity, and most of what we encounter in the world is perfectly simple."

You think so?

"Why else would I say it? What possible motive could I have? I'm not trying to impress anyone."

And I am? Whom am I trying to impress?

"Everyone. Yourself, first of all. First you deceive yourself and then you suppose you can fool the world. Or even worse, you think you have succeeded. Which makes you king of the universe. But look around you, at this small, bare room, your utilitarian table, the somewhat grimy panes of the window at which you spend so much time. Have you ever thought of cleaning them? It isn't at all difficult. But it would be beneath you, I suppose, as a king."

Are you trying to be unpleasant?

"Certainly not. I don't have to try. You created me, after all. So these things I'm telling you have already occurred to you. It isn't up to me to think anything. My job is merely to give you permission to think more freely in a more spontaneous way."

Fine. I'll call you if I need you

He has no smart answer for that [Or none I could imagine.]

Pessoa refers to "the almost ecstatic pleasure of lying," and I consider this. Writers theoretically might take pleasure in untruths, which are fictions after all, in which their audiences believe, at least for a while. But fiction has no practical purpose, while lies can be malevolent. You forget to show up for some appointment and you claim to have left a message on the answering machine. The motive is to exculpate yourself, which is not honorable. Does that make the lie more pleasurable or less? Less, I think, because it is of a utilitarian rather than a purely esthetic purpose. Ferruccio would surely be impatient with so fine a distinction and he'd have lots of company but, as with all art, the details are everything.

Even among utilitarian untruths, there are gradations. "White lies" are not so bad. But the more serious lies ought to be distinguished—red, blue, Day-Glo orange, black, etc. And with these hues they taint the soul. If that were true, we might be more scrupulous. Or we might wind up with souls that resemble Jackson Pollock paintings. No one would know, of course. And that would constitute yet another lie.

We are all haunted by the memory of a crime we have either committed or wanted to. Shrewdly the church exploits this guilt that is a part of our character— even of those who are not guilty. Confessions, penances, and offerings hold out a hope of remission—not of our sins but our feelings of sinfulness. Let him who is without sin congratulate himself for his sanity.

Is this what I think? The question has never posed itself so bluntly to me before. It could be me speaking, but it could also be Reis or Soares, using me as their agent. I have no way of knowing. There can be evidence of authenticity—when I find errors or awkwardness in what I have written. As scholars say in their modest acknowledgements of help they have received from friends and colleagues, "the mistakes are my own."

If that is true, then the whole exercise of copy-editing is an effacing of personality. Correctness of orthography, grammer, and logic, is a hallmark of anonymity.

Did it occur to Pessoa that it would be witty to assign to each of his heteronymic figures a set of mistakes that would be part of his idiolect?

Perhaps not. But it could also be the case that he realized this posthumously and his spirit is taking advantage of the curious structure of this book to remedy that oversight. Or at least to admit it to us.

Ferruccio raises an eyebrow. He doesn't say anything for a while, but then he sighs again and decides to intrude.

"You remember, don't you, that your father used to say, 'You will be a writer when you have a story to tell.'"

"He's right. My father used to say that. It pains me to remember it because it was a demonstration of his lack of understanding of what I do. And it is incidentally nonsensical. I can reverse it and suggest that when I am a writer I will have a story to tell. Stories don't make writers; writers make stories."

"Don't distract me. The trouble you have recalling this is that a part of you knows he was right. You dislike it, but narrative is a part of writing. It isn't vulgar or out of fashion. People are still interested in what happens and then what happens next, and why. You'd rather not go there, but that doesn't make you more refined or intelligent, does it?"

"I don't think so."

"Of course you do. If I think so, where must I be getting the thought? I may have expressed it but it is still yours."

I am not going to argue. The way the game seems to be played, I can't possibly win. In any event, there is nothing I can learn from him that I do not already know.

There are people who have the knack of reading rapidly. You can watch them turning pages at an impressive, depressing rate. I think they don't read every word but scan down a page from the upper left to the lower right. I can't believe that they get every subtle nuance. So I don't envy them. Indeed, I worry sometimes that I am speed-reading my own life, which goes by at such a rate that I can't register it, let alone reflect on it. The unexamined life goes by too quickly for us to examine it.

Maybe back then there was less to do. Hanging around the agora and philosophizing makes fewer demands on our attention than smart phones and computers. On the other hand, they mostly lived shorter lives. We have antibiotics and insulin. But do we take advantage of these extra years? Not enough.

Sometimes when I am out walking, a phrase will occur to me that seems promising, but when I return home I have forgotten it. I feel foolish but I tell myself that my memory, acting as an editor, has rejected the phrase in order to spare me the frustration of working on it (playing with it) and having it come to nothing. It is for that reason that I choose not to carry a notebook and write these nuggets down. I'd be losing the collaboration of my forgetfulness that is so helpful to most of us.

A small notebook in my pocket could also be an admission of neediness. And of distrust, as if I expected these images and phrases not to occur to me anymore. Isn't that what my hoarding would imply?

To sit down at the table and unscrew the cap of the pen is to gamble, for sometimes you do well and sometimes you lose and have to crumple the paper and throw it into the wastebasket. Fair enough. But in casinos they eject the players who count cards, which the dealers consider to be cheating. Jotting things down in a notebook would be cheating, too.

This selective forgetfulness, or call it an editorial *Vergesslich- keit*, can occasionally make mistakes, discarding something that could have been of value. But then there is the possibility that the phrase or image will return—several times, if need be—as if in appeal from the first judgment. Each time there is an opportunity for me to reconsider what my brain has dismissed as worthless. Indeed, each reappearance of the seed of a thought makes it like- lier that I will recall it when I am at my writing table. One might even say that each apparition makes a deeper impression until it becomes annoying and the only way for me to rid myself of its pes- tering is for me to yield to its importunity and deal with it, writing something—or at least making the attempt.

Some of my best paragraphs have come into being in this mat- ter. I should probably be grateful, but I mostly have the feeling of having been bested and overwhelmed. I realize that this is an absurd reaction, but that thought neither protects me against the sense of defeat nor makes it go away. Absurdity, after all, is not an indication of falsity.

You will have noticed, if you are reading a conventional book, that the pages on your right have diminished almost to nothing (the nothingness Pessoa longed for?) which means that we are near the end. I should probably wave, bow, and disappear. But there is an observation I have made about the foregoing text. Some of these heteronymics seem to me more persuasive, more "real," than their colleagues. More vivid, anyway. Hegel's gnomic remark about how the real is the rational and the rational is the real is fun to play with. (It has to do with logical categories, I think.)

It would be closer to the truth to say that the real is the vivid and the vivid is the real.

If that is the case, then reality is not absolute but has gradations, a whole spectrum. And it then follows that vivid fictions (i. e. those that are well done) are more "real" than most of our actual lives, which tend to be tiresome and boring.

Medical ethicists and transplant surgeons wrangle about the difference between life and death (to which there are practical consequences), but discussions about the borderline between fact and fiction, reality and hypothesis, always seem frivolous.

But are they? Are they not as fundamental as the physician's quandary? More basic, even. We're talking about being and nothingness.

When God created the universe, was it worth the bother?

Reis doesn't actually die in Saramago's novel. Fictional characters don't die, so we should not be surprised. There is an enactment of a death, I suppose, for at the end Reis goes off with Pessoa, his creator—and Pessoa really is dead and has been since 1935. Except that Pessoa has become a fictional character, too, appearing as he does in Saramago's book. And this one.

Confusing? I think that was the intention. Magical realists (or realistic magicians) like confusion, which is an attempt to be truthful in fiction. Lies like truth? Non-being posing as being? Novels and stories exist in perilous, swampy ground. And if we confuse fact and fancy, befuddling our readers at least a little, we have not misled them. We have not lied. (But of course we have, although the readers know this. And they conspire.)

Fiction is an attempt at truth in another way, or was for Pessoa. He had no clear understanding of the boundary between internal and external reality, no certainty about what identity means, what it asserts, and what it denies. His uncertainties were, for him, the fundamental truths of both fiction and life. Uncertainty was exactly what he was trying to convey.

Trying? No, succeeding, I would say. His success was so great that most other fiction seems contrived and suspicious. Even worse, most experience seems similarly suspicious. The day is clear. The sky is blue. The grass is green. We bring to this landscape our own mists, blurring everything with our own biographies and their eccentricities and imprecisions. This sounds bad, but we can learn to be proud of ourselves, for each man has his own blur— that is his identity.

Over the years, my face in the mirror has changed, with my skin sagging, the hair on my head turning white, and the pouches under my eyes getting larger. What is unchanging, and therefore as close to the truth as we can come, is the mirror itself, with its minute flaws and consequent distortions. Accept the distortions and learn to take pride in them, and you have taken at least a step on the path to wisdom. (If indeed there is any such thing as wisdom let alone a path to it. Okay, the feeling of being wise, which is as close as we are likely to come, either in this life or the shadowy existence into which Saramago has Pessoa leading the compliant Dr. Reis.)

FIM

ABOUT THE AUTHOR

DAVID R. SLAVITT was born in White Plains, New York. He earned a BA in 1956 from Yale, graduating magna cum laude, and an MA from Columbia in 1957. He has since authored more than 120 books of poetry, literary fiction, pulp fiction, memoir, criticism, and translation. He has translated texts from Latin, Greek, Hebrew, Greenlandic, French, Italian, and Spanish, including *The Metamorphoses of Ovid* and *The Book of the Twelve Prophets*, as well as works by Sophocles, Horace, Seneca, Dante, Boethius, Marie de France, and others. Slavitt is the recipient of numerous awards, including a National Endowment for the Arts fellowship for translation, an award for literature from the American Academy and Institute of Arts and Letters, and a Rockefeller Foundation artist's residency at Bellagio. He currently lives in Cambridge, Massachusetts.

www.ingramcontent.com/pod-product-compliance
Lightning Source LLC
Chambersburg PA
CBHW020639250626
47154CB00008B/2744